THE ATHEIST
and other stories

THE ATHEIST
and other stories

Seán Mac Mathúna

WOLFHOUND PRESS

Published in Great Britain 1988
© 1987 Seán Mac Mathúna

This book is published with the financial assistance of The Arts Council/ An Chomhairle Ealaíon, Ireland.

First published in Ireland, in 1987 by
WOLFHOUND PRESS
68 Mountjoy Square,
Dublin 1.

British Library Cataloguing in Publication Data

Mac Mathúna, Seán
    The atheist: 15 short stories
    I. Title
    891.6'234 [F]   PB1399.M22/

    ISBN 0 86327 102 2

Acknowledgement is made to the *Irish Press*, *The Irish Times*, *Best Irish Writing I & II* (Paul Elek) and other journals where some of these stories have been published.

Cover design by Jan de Fouw
Typesetting by Redsetter Limited
Printed by Billings & Sons, Worcester

Contents

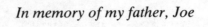

In memory of my father, Joe

The Queen of Killiney

Dinny Long, TD, was too wise to get married and too young to recognise the pain of loneliness. At forty-four, his name was as familiar to his constituents as was their brand of cornflakes, Land Rover, or cure for scour in cattle. He had an intense feeling for geography. He lived within thirty yards of his constituency boundary, and he knew that if he lived any closer, his constituents would accuse hom of trying to escape. He lived close enough to Dublin to visit his mistress twice a week and far away enough to be safe from the marauding hordes of scavengers when the country had a debt of 40 billion and the dole would be stopped.

He was busy; but sometimes busy became hectic and hectic became insane. Then he withdrew to Bowlawling House, Georgian Residence, c. 300 acres plus eight loose boxes – home. And his housekeeper, Kitty, who could charm away callers as well as she could jug a hare. But they still pursued him up the gravel drive, on foot, bikes, mercs and now and again an oddity on a horse. 'Mercs are the worst, they walk down on you,' said Kitty. They almost did, pushing past her, saying firmly, 'Tell Mr. Long it's only a minute.'

It never was. It was an eternity of 'Swing this for me and I'll canvass for you' or worse, 'Swing this for me for I canvassed for you'. It was all a litany of supplication that dulled his mind, and which he barely acknowledged by nodding at the pauses. Humanity had become transparent. In an ironic moment he had the idea of getting a badge with 'Support your local swinger' written on it, but Sambo said no, it would only draw them on. When things really got bad, Dinny sought out the damp quiet of the cellars in Bowlawling. They were filled with the remnants of former occupants. In such moments he leafed through old diaries, fingered books spotted with mould, and closing his eyes drew their antique fragrance deep within him. If ever he were free he would bottle the smell of old books and hawk it through the world to lost romantics. And photographs. A woman, a parasol, in the doorway of Bowlawling, smiling, all washed in the sepia of eternity. Scrawled on the back with surging flourish 'Remember Ballskarney! Love for ever, Rodney'. In such moments he would press the object to his heart and whisper 'Maybe I do love humanity after all'.

But out of the cellars he had to come, into the bright insanity of day. And that meant Sambo. Dinny walked into the clinic in Rathgrew. Sambo had his kinky snakeskin boots on the desk. 'Howdy Pal, just havin' me some shut-eye. Git off your feet and have a seat.' 'Sambo,' said Dinny, standing in the middle of the clinic, 'this place is looking more and more like the O.K. Corral.' Sambo drew on a large Havana and blew a smoke-ring towards the ceiling. 'Gawd damn, Dinny, you're real hornery, guess it's gonna be one o' them days.'

Dinny eyed the walls of the clinic – a paradox of posters advertising Sambo Reilly as a Bronco Buster, a cowpoke, a gambler on a Mississippi sternwheeler, a laster of nine seconds on a Texas Longhorn, all set against the posters of the Pro-life campaign. Nowhere did the name Dinny Long appear; more and more Sambo was taking over the clinic. This suited Dinny. 'Sambo, I don't mind you wearing a stetson because you have a face only a mother could love. It adds a bit of class – the cigar some flavour, but the spurs I object to. You're my election agent, secretary, fender-offer of *gaeilgeoirí*. I need you but you're trying to escape into a western. Spurs out.' Sambo didn't move. He pulled the brim of his stetson down to the half-moons of his eyes and lay back farther on the swivel. 'Folks agettin' kinda nasty about mah face. Waal, ah guess there must be sumpin to it – guy rode into town yistahday, said I got a face like a corduroy trousers – gal way down Tucson way tells me ah got a face like an unmade bed.' Slowly he eased his boots onto the ground and removed the spurs. 'Dollar ninety-five – Maceys – only plastic.'

Sambo filled him in on the goings on. Dinny was president, secretary, patron, committee member of so many bodies that he needed help. Sambo told him what funerals should be attended, weddings, christenings. But above all, he'd have to go down to the Rathgrew Community School, where he was chairman of the Board of Management. Detta Hearne, the Principal, needed him fast. 'The old gal's in a flap.'

And then the Amendment Campaign. Dinny eyed a number of placards that Sambo had made with markers. There was no 'double M' in amendment. It didn't matter, said Sambo, folks didn't care whether he was illiterate or not, they were all raring to vote against abortion. It was important that Dinny be associated with that response. The whole constituency was ninety-five percent Catholic farmers. But Dinny looked after everybody – Catholic, Protestant and Atheist. The Atheist's name was Tom Ruddy and he snarled about God, Ethiopia and the price of drink.

Dinny felt dynamic and grabbed a hammer and nails and began to nail placards to the battens. Suddenly he stopped and said 'Sambo, this is the way Christianity started.' 'How boss?' 'With a hammer and nails.' He paused in thought for a moment and then continued to hammer. Manual labour of the monotonous kind eased his mind.

'Boss waddya think o' this abortion business?' Dinny paused again. 'Sambo my father told me once – in this politics business you don't think, you interpret. If I start thinking, I'm out of a job in the morning.' Sambo wanted to know what he meant. Dinny was a thinker. Things stuck in his throat, especially in the Dáil. But they always vanished, not into thin air but into his thin blood. Thinner and thinner.

The typewriter clicked; it was time to leave. Sambo had recently discovered its magic. Any moment the questions would start – spell this, spell that, a nicotined finger waiting for the answers. Dinny needed Sambo's flamboyance to flood him with votes and that was all. But sometimes Sambo went too far. If he was caught personating again, Dinny would have to give him a dressing down. Anyone in the constituency would know that face boiled in porridge.

Click, click. Dinny headed for the door. 'I'm going to need you Sunday night at the concert, bound to be a gaeilgeoir problem.' Dinny didn't hate Irish. He even had one sentence – *Vótáil Donncha Ó Longaigh, Uimh. 1*. He knew that in Irish all the four-lettered words were three-lettered – fifteen in German – and that there were only three ways to have Irish. One, to be born into it; two, to pretend to have it; three, to have a ventriloquist. As he wasn't a hypocrite he rejected the second, but sometimes toyed with the third. Sambo had a way of putting a pint into a gaeilgeoir's hand, and a way of talking pure Cowpoke without subjunctives that stilled all linguistic differences. On his way out, he picked from a shelf a copy of the Irish Constitution, *Bunreacht na hÉireann*, and stuffed it into his pocket. Seeing as they were going to amend the Constitution, he might as well read the damn thing.

Down at the community school, Detta Hearne ruled with an iron fist. Her office was decorated with posters of babies and tiny tots, all proclaiming the sanctity of life. On the wall behind her was a huge replica of a voting paper. VOTE X TÁ / YES TO PROTECT LIFE. She explained rapidly that he would be chairing the appointments board – and that there was a certain young lady part-time on the staff who had a good chance of getting the job. Detta wanted her stopped; out. She had recently been to England. Her health had improved immensely since that visit. Did Dinny understand? He nodded. She was also a member of the following organisations: Well-Woman's Centre, AIM, Women's Right to Choose, Rape Crisis Centre, Women's Political Association and the A.F.M.F.W. 'No way is she wanted here. She is trouble with a big T.' It was important that it happen today, because the girl was not beyond using influence.

Dinny tried to argue, but it was no use. Who else would be on the Board? Old political friends – Joe Heaslip, Cecil Falvey, Tadhg MacCarthy. And Seosamh O Mianain. He was just one of the staff. She'd take care of him. She ranted on about the Fight, the Glory. Dinny found himself twisting *Bunreacht na hÉireann* in his hands. She was going to have a great school. There were the Brothers up the road and the convent down the road and by God she'd drive both of them to the wall yet. Her lips snipped the words like scissors.

Dinny did what he was told. It was easy. The girl in question was in temperament identical to Detta. She had enough fire in her soul to set any school ablaze. She'd get a job somewhere else, he felt, as he crossed her name off the list. Afterwards, as he walked the gravel with Tadhg Mac to the car, their footsteps sounding like chewing horses, Tadhg said: 'Did you get the irony? If the girl aborts – no job. If she has the baby - still no job.' At the door of his car Dinny paused. 'The structure of society is a flimsy thing – it is vulnerable, a stand must be made.' He fell into the seat.

Things lingered on – wrong things in his mind. It was time for Jenny. Jenny was his favourite person, a roan Irish hunter who never answered him back. Although, once she had thrown him on the lawn, and the Chief standing on the steps of Bowlawling. He had raged at her: 'Jenny, you thundering fart, you whore out of the knackers' yard, may you never foal again.' But the Chief had said it was alright, he fell off his horse too. Today, he allowed her to take him all the way across the fields to Faarness Wood. He threw himself upon the ground, listening to Jenny champ stray grass among the shadows. He watched the trees release the clouds one by one, by one. He searched his pockets for *Bunreacht na hÉireann*. He must have left it in the school.

Dinny loved Dublin, the freedom of a city where you could drink a pint without having your hand pumped by someone on the take, get a hamburger without being set upon by swingsters. He avoided the Stroke Triangle between Mount Street, Stephen's Green and Dublin Castle like the plague. Even Sambo agreed: 'Only Billy the Kid would go in there and come out with his hat on.' Sometimes when the whip was on, he had to go to the Dáil. He disliked it. He had made his maiden speech there a long time ago, on scwerage schemes. He had worn a blue pinstripe mohair suit with a rose in his buttonhole. Sealy, the political correspondent, who made TDs crawl all the way to Slea Head, had seen some irony in this and dubbed him 'Dinny the Swank'. It had stuck. His opponent in Rathgrew, Jack Halloran, who, according to polls, was narrowing the gap between them, had dubbed him 'Swing-along Dinny'. It was Jack Halloran that Dinny feared. Jack had beaten him to the Rathlickey disaster, where 40 pigs were drowned. Jack Halloran was shown in *The Post*, standing, hat off, beside the trailer of dead pigs, a solemn look on his face. 'Halloran is as slow as the second coming of Christ,' was Sambo's verdict, however.

The freedom of Neasa's flat always overwhelmed Dinny. It was home not just because he paid for it; it was a safe house in good or bad times. And Neasa a beauty – he only went for beautiful women. She was also vivacious. 'Do you like me in this, should I wear pink – will the blue go with this? How about black? Are we going to the

Dáil restaurant? Will Jamsey be there, and Finnegan. They're great crack. How's Sambo, I have cigars for him. Who's this Kitty? Why is she always gone when I go down? I could do Kitty's job better. I'm great with people.' Dinny told her that with a face like hers, she'd only draw them on. She should see Kitty's face. Would he like to have dinner or did he want to go to bed now? She had chilli with red and green peppers – she had wine. He wasn't drinking. The blinds killed the sunshine and turned her bed to rose. He didn't just love her, he needed her. Only he knew that. And he'd have to marry her. Only she knew that.

He crossed Killiney Hill to his brother, Paddy, parish priest of Tigraskin. They were in his sitting room. 'Why can't you have a brandy, just one?' Dinny wouldn't. 'This place reminds me of my clinic – no sign of God in it.' He glanced around the room, strewn with spears, flints, skulls and photographs of digs. 'This room is for me brother, and as for God, God is everywhere. No need to remind him,' said Paddy, cupping his brandy in his hands. 'You'd have made a great politician,' said Dinny. 'There's very little difference' was the reply. And then, 'Come up to Killiney Hill with me before it gets dark.'

'You still rootin' up there?'

Paddy said he was. He had discovered something. His eyes twinkled. But it had to be before it got dark.

They stood in the wood of Killiney Hill. It was a tangle of light and leafy shadows. Paddy stood in a glade and pointed out the three large stones. They were boundaries. 'Of what?' asked Dinny. 'Come,' said Paddy, 'look!' He pressed a spade into the turf and levered it back to reveal a widening crack. Dinny peered in. 'What is it, a bone some dog buried?' 'No, it's an infant's skull.' Dinny felt a shiver pass through him, going somewhere fast. Paddy told him it was a *Cillíneach*, a graveyard for unbaptised infants and aborted foetuses. In Irish they said 'as lonely as a *Cillíneach*'. No man could go in at night. Women were free. The dead had their power and the underprivileged dead the greatest power of all. 'To the people who live near here, Killiney Hill is but some rocks, some trees and a place for the dog to piss – they holiday in Spain, work in the city and drink in Dalkey – the media has swamped their souls – but the magic of Killiney waits – woe to those who tread on the magic of Killiney.'

The shadows were getting too long. They would have to go.

Back in the sitting room they talked some more. 'You talk like a pagan,' said Dinny. 'God loves pagans too,' replied Paddy. 'Superstition is wrong, it doubts the love of God,' said Dinny.

'You'd have made a good priest,' said Paddy.

They talked into the night. Dinny decided to walk over the hill to Neasa's flat. The night was dark. Late closers had cleared. The night was still. He could barely make out the path through the trees. Then he lost it and stumbled on. Suddenly he was in the glade. He stood at the boundary and looked in. He did not believe. He walked into the middle. Nothing, just the moon and all the stars. He pressed on until he saw a light through the trees. It was some kind of hotel. The moon shone on its sign-board: 'The Queen of Killiney. Open to Non-Residents'. He had never heard of it. Curiosity made him mount the steps. He stopped and listened. Something was wrong. He couldn't hear the city traffic. He pushed the door and entered a bar foyer. It was tasteful. 'Just like I'd design it myself,' he muttered.

'Were you talking to me?' said a voice full of laughter. In the shadow he saw a woman. As she moved into the light, he thought there was something familiar about her. But when she came up close, he knew.

'Incredible!' he said, ' – you're the spitting image of Jean Simmons.'

She stopped in front of him, her eyes glassy with pleasure. 'Is that good or bad?' she asked, wetting her lips.

'The best,' he said. 'She was always my favourite actress, even more than Ursula Andress.'

'What was *she* like?' she asked, with fluttering eyelashes.

He looked into eyes that were the colour of faded jeans. She blushed slightly under his gaze, dropped her eyes, raised them again quizically, brushed a lock of hair and smiled. 'Ursula Andress is magnetic in an animal kind of way – sullen, demanding.'

'Go on,' said the girl.

'She radiates desire but never peace. She'd need a lion-tamer or weight-lifter or something.'

'I know what you mean,' she said, 'I'm not like that.'

'Not in a million years,' he said, looking into her sky-blue wells.

He thought of Jean Simmons, gorgeously frail, helpless and alone, always waiting to be rescued. Dependent beautiful Jean who couldn't buy a drink for herself or cross the road. If he were married to her, he would gladly spend his life buttering her bread and peeling her potatoes.

Suddenly he was aware that he was still staring into her eyes. He thought of Neasa and excused himself. 'I've got to go.' She looked at him with disappointment, her fingers twisting the corner of her blouse. 'Please don't go yet. Stay and have a drink. It's lonely here, the hotel hasn't opened yet.'

'By Christ, I *will* have a drink – a big brandy and fast,' he heard himself saying. The girl radiated so much wellbeing that he felt himself re-charging.

She brought a huge drink to the fireplace and taking his arm, led him to a chair. Her hand excited him so much she could have pushed him off a cliff. She placed a pillow behind his head, and this made his toes open and shut. He began to relax so much he could hear the hiss. She sat beside him on a foot stool. He looked down at her dress and could have sworn it was the one she wore in *The Big Country*. 'Do you go to films?' he asked. No, she said, she was an orphan and knew nobody. Her name was Macha. It was lonely on the hill at night. She leaned over and whispered into his ear that twigs snapping in the scrub frightened her at night.

The glow of her breath in his ear and the proximity of her mouth made springs go twang within him. He looked down at the curve of her firm thigh very much at home in her *Big Country* dress. When he had finished his drink and she asked him to see her as far as her door, which was down at the end of a long corridor, it seemed natural to say yes.

At the door she paused and said, 'Come in a minute.' All he noticed was the black bedsheets trimmed in scarlet, colours he had once seen on his cousins panties and which remained in his mind as symbols of carnality. But there was no need for symbols, for the real thing was in his arms and the ancient heritage of man ruled.

One morning a month later, Dinny Long got sick in the clinic. Sambo said, 'Boss, you been hittin' the booze again.' Dinny looked as frail as a shadow in a bottle. He just shook his head at Sambo and said, 'Christ.' After a week of his getting sick, Sambo was convinced it wasn't booze. 'You gotta see Doc Holiday, Dinny, fast.'

Séamus Cridden listened to the symptoms: 44 years old, sick, would like to be young again. 'Male menopause – classic symptoms,' said Séamus. He prescribed a track suit and a tonic and to send Kitty up to him. As he departed, Séamus called after him, 'If it isn't that, you're pregnant!' His laughter followed Dinny all the way to the car.

He looked fine in his plum track suit, except for the middle-age spread the doctor had mentioned. Once while jogging in Killiney, he searched for The Queen of Killiney. Nothing but briars, heather and rocks. He stood at the Obelisk looking out to sea, his eyes clouded, seagulls drifting through his dreams.

One night he awoke. He called for Kitty. 'Have we any blackberry jam in the house?' 'No, but we have gooseberry, lemon curd and pear flan.' 'I want some blackberry jam and I want it now.' Kitty put on her coat and went looking for blackberry jam. Nothing surprised her.

Dinny asked Paddy about the hotel. 'No such hotel – Heights, Castle and Court, but no Queen.'

'Even in the past?'

'Negative. You look in poor shape, you should see a doctor.'

'Has there ever been a Queen of Killiney in this dark world and wide?' he wailed. 'No sir, never been – I'm the historian – you sure you won't have a drink? No, never been a place like that. Only Queen of Killiney I ever heard about was Macha.'

Dinny Long bundled himself out of the sofa and stood bolt upright so fast that Paddy was taken aback. 'You either take a drink or I call a doctor.' He poured the drink carefully and passed it to Dinny. 'Fella called Léinín, sixth century. Had five daughters: Druigan, Euigen, Luicill, Riomthach and Macha – five saints, feast day 6th of March. They built the old church in Killiney which still stands – hence the name Killiney, which means the church of the daughters of Léinín. The awful people who live around here never spare a thought for those girls. Macha was beautiful and called the Queen.'

'Did she look like Jean Simmons?'

Paddy smiled. 'You should drink more often. See – you're getting your sense of humour back. No, we haven't a snap of her. All I know is she's the patron saint of stillborn, unbaptised and aborted children.' He looked at his brother, a frail thing in the embrace of a wing chair. He was pale and remote.

'Do you believe in magic?' Dinny asked.

'God is magic.'

'I thought magic was the dark end of the spectrum.'

'God created the spectrum.'

'But – '

Dinny pulled the cord over his bed. He had never done it before. Kitty came in a nightdress. 'Any peaches in the house?' he asked. 'I'm dying for a spoon of peaches.' 'No – ' she said, 'but you never ate the blackberry jam. Will you have a spoonful of that?'

He grew fatter and depressed. One morning as he was shaving, something kicked him in the belly. He dropped the razor and backed all the way into the shower. He placed his hand on his stomach; then it kicked again. 'Crucified Jesus! Kitty, come up here fast!' he roared. She came tearing in. 'Jesus – I'm terrified, something is moving in my stomach.' She made him sit on the bath and ran her hand expertly over the swelling. 'Get down on your knees and throw your head back.' He did so, and all the while, the hand on his stomach. She made him go on all fours, take a deep breath and hold it. He did. Shortly, she told him to get up. 'What's wrong with me?' he whined. 'It's only the baby,' she said.

For a long time he stared at her, and then he began to fall like a tree. She caught him in time and dragged him to his bed. When he was tucked in he began to wail. 'I'm a man – how could I have a baby?' She fussed around the room. 'Look,' she said, 'I was midwife in this parish for twenty years. That's what they all said. "How could I be pregnant?" From the way it's sitting, I'd say it's a girl.'

'I love God,' said Dinny. 'Why would he do this to me? If it's a baby, how do we get it out?'

Kitty was hanging his clothes in the wardrobe. 'No problem getting it out. What I'd like to know is how did it get in. Do you want those peaches? The place below is filling up with stuff. Do you want them?' 'No. But I want the bottle of Redbreast, and I want it fast.'

'No drink, bad for the baby, no pills, aspros, or tobacco.'

Suddenly he sat up. 'You wouldn't tell Sambo or Séamus Cridden? If word gets out, I'm ruined. I can make you rich. I'm in the agri business. I have shares in pubs and hotels from here to Helvick Head. Sure you won't tell anyone?'

'Nobody would believe it,' she said as she closed the door quietly.

He took to his bed, refused to go out, refused visitors. Word got out that he was dying. His opponent Jack Halloran called the whole thing 'Long D's journey into night' in *The Post*. The throng at the door kept Kitty going all day. Every second hour he called her up to make sure that it wasn't a phantom, air, something he ate, or a baby. When she pronounced it a baby, he wailed and thumped the pillows. On the way downstairs, she'd mutter about having two babies on her hands. All this fuss over a perfect pregnancy.

Kitty brought him every medical book she could find. He spent days going over the reproductive system. The whole thing was a mess. From the fallopian tubes to the vulva was a crazy plumbing system of nooks and crannies. He thanked the Lord he was a man. Then he remembered the baby and he sank into the pillows. Kitty stuck her head in the door. 'Do you want those apricots?'

Paddy brought the bishop, who put his hand on the bulge. 'Liver,' he said. 'French liver, gets very big, seen it in Avignon.' Dinny shook his head. 'Tell him Paddy.' Paddy said he didn't drink at all.

'Not a drop, at all, at all,' said the bishop. 'That's bad, makes a man mean and cranky. Then it's gluttony.' 'No, I hardly eat anything, not even blackberry jam or bloody apricots.' Paddy told the bishop it was true, that he had become quite ascetic.

'He's dying so,' said the bishop. 'Would you like to go to St Clement's?' Dinny shook his head vigorously. 'St Clement's is for the living dead,' he snarled. 'The living dead should be damn glad they're alive,' retorted the bishop. He gave Dinny his blessing and moved on to the next tragedy in the queue.

The Chief came to visit Dinny. Sambo waited outside the door, while they whispered inside. 'Sambo won't work for anybody 'cept you,' said the Chief, trying to persuade Dinny to change his mind.

'Then let Sambo work for himself – he'll do it hands down,' said Dinny. The Chief gulped, looked at the door and thought aloud, 'Jesus, Sambo?' Dinny felt himself laughing, but the baby stirred.

Sambo would head the poll. His maiden speech would be a eulogy on Jesse James. Buswell's would stock his favourite cigars.

'Who can I turn to for help Kitty?' he begged. 'Try these – ' and she dropped some women's magazines on a tray. Knitting patterns; 'Is your husband jealous of your baby?'; 'Knit your own babygro'; 'Diet for Mums.'

Neasa came. Dinny sank into the blankets. 'Don't come near me, stay five yards away from me.' Neasa stood three yards away. 'Is it one of these transmitted diseases?' 'No – ' said Dinny, 'just contagious. Stay away from me.'

It was Neasa's visit that did it. The courage and immorality of desperation brought him in a taxi to the Liberties in Dublin. He knocked at a house in Protestant Row. An old woman answered. 'I've got business for you,' said Dinny, as he pushed his way in, ' – a girl in trouble.'

'If it's that kind of trouble, forget it, after what they did to that poor nurse.'

Dinny remembered. They had hanged her.

'This girl is rich.'

The woman hesitated. 'How rich?'

'Three thousand pounds.'

'For that kind of money, we'd do an elephant. I'll send for Mena.'

'Who's Mena?'

'Mena's for special tricks. Have your girl here at seven o'clock tonight.'

He spent the day around Camden Street, Wexford Street and in the back streets off St Patrick's Cathedral. He noted the shabbiness of the houses – the poverty of the people – and yet their happiness. He was no longer a man. Nor a woman. He was a hunted animal. Yet he was discovering himself, discovering humanity.

He was at the door at 7 pm sharp. 'Where's the girl?' 'She'll be along – she's shy.' Cold sweat was breaking out on his forehead. 'I want to see the place first.' They took him into a room in which there was a large tub in the middle of the floor. Beside it was a large electric boiler, bubbling. He eyed it suspiciously. On the table was a large bottle of CDC gin. He looked from the bath to the gin. He had read *Saturday Night and Sunday Morning*. And the revulsion returned. 'How much gin?' he asked. 'The lot,' they said. 'That way boiling water might move it.' He hated gin. 'What's the sawdust on the floor for?' Mena came forward to the table and opened a large box. She took out a needle as big and curved as a coat hanger. She held it up, gleaming in the light.

'How?' he asked.

'How do you think?' she said.

He felt his sphincter muscle close like a door in a storm. Quickly he dug into his pockets and pulled out a fistful of notes and flung them on the table. 'She changed her mind,' he said leaving quickly and escaping into the clamour of Dublin's streets.

All night he spent walking the back streets off the Quays – Lotts, Great Strand Street, Liffey Street – there nobody knew him. The depressed and defeated found comfort in back streets. At twelve o'clock, black Liffey waters swelling from Ringsend, many, many mouthfuls. A ship, a man, somebody's newspaper flapping at his feet, unlit stores. Three more inches to eternity. He couldn't swim – it would be fast. But his body washed up in Sandymount – the autopsy would find the child. Christ, he'd be in the Guinness Book of Records. His relatives would curse his name. He staggered back into a dockside doorway. If only he were a woman, he would gladly drown himself, herself.

'You okay?' It was an elderly garda.

'Yeah – just looking for a parishioner of mine.' He passed himself off as a priest effortlessly. 'A girl.'

'She on the make – sailors?'

'No, just pregnant.'

'They all go to England now 'cept the very young and frightened.' He stamped his feet against the chill. 'Time was we hauled out three a week from Alexandra Basin – poor little drowned rags of things.' He stamped his feet again and left.

He took the boat to Liverpool. It took some time with directories before he found the expensive private clinic, east of the city, that he knew would do. He slunk in for the appointment like a thieving dog.

The room was opulent, more like a film set for a period drama, and the consultant's cultured mildness matched the scene. He wasn't in the least perturbed that the patient was male. Such genetic quirks were quite fascinating, but of course it would cost double. Or would he like to have the child perhaps, and put it up for adoption? And give it a name. Most Irish girls called them either Patrick or Mary. Dinny took fright at the suggestion. Such a thing would damage his career. And then he remembered he didn't have a career. He was finished with all that sordidness.

'I'm afraid I shall have to ask you to proceed with the, the – '

'Abortion?'

'The operation.'

'Yes, there's a great comfort in words.'

They offered him a local anaesthetic but he asked to be knocked out, as it was a caesarian. When he awoke, there was group of white-coated surgeons all around his bed.

'Is it over – ?' he croaked.

'Yes.' They said.

'Is it – ?'

'Dead?' said one. 'Alive?' said another.

'No, it is not alive,' said somebody.

He felt a lump in his throat. The enormity of it all got to him. He felt loss.

'Who'd want to be a woman?'

'In Ireland.' They added.

'Was it a boy or girl?'

They looked at him for a long time in silence. Then one of them beckoned to a nurse. She came forward, pushing a trolley to the bedside. This sent him under the bedclothes in terror. But they insisted that he look. He raised his head and looked at the trolley for a long time. It was a copy of the Irish Constitution, greatly enlarged. The doctors pointed to the words on the cover – *Bunreacht na hÉireann* – and asked what it meant.

'It is meaningless,' he answered in a far away voice.

Wedge

The white host descending on her pink tongue, that was her colour scheme, the way I saw her. The others in the congregation saw her differently, their eyes dismembering her at the altar rails, their hearts' desires sifting through the pieces for what they never had, or lost or dreamed of: hair, hands, clothes, body, eyes, the way she walked, the way she spoke, the way she didn't have to speak.

She handed me the keys of the Volvo that morning. I drove the car out of the church grounds without a crash of gears and gunned it down the road. I was almost doing the ton as we passed Three Mile House, but the squad passed us and I had to make a quick change at Cloon bridge. That's when I noticed the mark on her neck. 'What happened your neck?' Her fingers did a nervous dance on the collar of her blouse. The bruise looked like a thunderhead on a clear sky.

'It's nothing, dear, nothing for you to worry about.'

This made me feel uncomfortable.

'It looks ugly, what happened?'

Her eyes took on a dreamy remoteness, her hands transferring to the wheel, her index finger tapping out uncertain morse on the rim.

'Last night was particularly bad, he was very drunk.'

I felt myself getting very angry.

'Did he hit you?'

By this time the bruise was completely hidden in white lace.

'Don't get involved in this, Eamonn, this is adult stuff. Things will get better, they usually do, you'll see. Just as long as nobody comes between us. Say nothing, do you understand?'

Her voice had the kind of intonation that made shorty work of male aggression. She explained that all she wanted was for me to be her confidant. I loved it. She put a ten pound note into my breast pocket and said that I could buy us all a drink up at the Grove, and maybe take a few minutes at the wheel on the way home.

Up in the Grove Hotel my mother had a pink gin with Rodney Barcastle. Rodney who is full of charm and snappy repartee. And horses. He would spend days talking horses. I confess to being very impressed by this horsey set, the way they put you out of countenance when looking at you, the way they greet barmaids, the way they drink, not in gulps, but just the right amount, the way they pitch life into the boot of a Saab Turbo. I listened to Dick Roche, the vet, talk about Swiss francs out of the corner of his mouth and I watched my mother stand chatting in the bay window with Rodney. The sunlight always fell on my mother, on her golden hair, on her blue eyes, on her pink gin and through her dress, revealing her thighs in silhouette to the whole room. But nobody seemed to mind.

My father loved wood, loved to see it grow, to see it felled, to see it split. He only relaxed when you put an axe into his hands. He would fill his lungs with the scent of freshly-felled timber and place his finger on a precise spot in the cut and say 'The air and rain that gave life and sustenance to that part of the tree did likewise for me when I came back from South Africa.' He felt related to timber, he said.

I looked at the chaos of felled trees, split trunks and logs and the scatter of loppings, and I marvelled at the energy that could create so much havoc in a quiet corner of woodland. I gave him tea in a flask, which he drank, his Adam's apple dislocating with each gulp. He sat on a log and lit a cigarette. He held the smoke in his lungs, one eye shut to aid the satisfaction. 'The time is up for all the elms. There is no escape from the Dutch disease. It's the best wood for paling, resistant to rot. Nothing to beat it for coffins. Next big wind will knock enough elms to make coffins for us all.' He looked at me. 'Where've you been this morning?'

I recounted the morning's doings.

'You two are getting around a lot lately.'

I searched his face and thought I discovered mockery around his eyes. I thought of my mother's frail beauty.

'She's my mother, she needs my help. Any objections?'

I said it with just the right amount of defiance to make him back off. He looked at me for some time and then spat on his hands.

'How would you fancy a splitting session? I've got some new wedges, elm wedges. Ever hear the old proverb, "Wedge of elm to split the elm."?'

He stood the wedges while I tapped them into the tiny cracks on the trunk, then hammered them stoutly. There was an ominous thud as wood ground against wood and then a slow deep rending of timber.

'Mind the way you drive the wedge or it will skine and come at you at a hundred miles an hour and smash your jaw to smithereens.'

He was full of old words, old sayings, old beliefs: he was afraid of beetles, red-haired women and whistling after dark.

I got fed up with hammering wedges. I left my father fondling logs, searching for the natural lines of weakness. Christ, how a man can turn his back upon the whole world and skulk in a corner of wood beats me.

I was doing Leaving Cert Maths in the library when I heard fingers tapping on the french windows. It was Joe Hassett, my father's drinking partner. Shock waves of tension always preceded him in our house. He had long ago forsaken the dialect of words for that of the wink and nudge. I let him in. He raised an eyebrow towards the hall.

'She's in the kitchen,' I said.

He then nodded towards the lawn.

'He's in the orchard.'

He glanced down at the maths, nudged me in the ribs, winked twice, placed a finger conspiratorially to his lips and tiptoed out of the library. Christ deliver me from winkers is all I can say. I couldn't write another thing. I felt my forearms grow tense. Neighs of laughter came from the orchard. Shortly I heard Joe's Granada purr down the avenue. They were going to Downey's. They never went to the Grove.

Mother and I had dinner together, the clink of cutlery on china only emphasising the heavy silence. When we finished she dabbed her mouth daintily and said tight-lipped: 'Tonight has all the signs of being a bad night.' Her voice was shaking.

'By Christ, it will not be a bad night.' And I thumped the table and made the candles flicker.

She raised her hand and said there was enough aggression in the house already. 'I thought we had agreed you're my confidant,' she whispered, 'somebody reliable and strong.'

When she spoke to me like that it gave me a funny feeling, made me feel sort of secure. She poured coffee, milked and sugared it for me. Then she stirred it, her eyes lost in the swirl. She passed it to me.

'What bothers me is that the drink is going to kill him some night.'

'How?'

'I'm not sure. I keep thinking of the shaky bridge. It's bad enough when you're sober.' Sometimes my father crossed the little suspension bridge over the Flesk in full winter spate, black, silent, its two banks straining against its wet power. I thought of my father floating in it, his mouth filling with cold Flesk, his childlike eyes staring in wonder at the magic of bridges.

The commotion, shouting and door-banging wakened me, then my father's drunken speech. She banged the door in Joe Hassett's face, hunted me back to bed and tried to calm my father. I lay between the sheets as tense as a plank of wood, listening to the rise and fall of their voices until I finally fell asleep.

I awoke with a guilty start, knowing that I was too late for school. She was standing in the middle of the room with a cup of tea for me. She had a black eye, her hair was dishevelled, there was not a trace of the glamorous woman save the silk dressing-gown.

'I'm going to fix this business once and for all,' I said, reaching for my trousers.

But she grabbed me by the elbow and pressed me back on the pillow. 'We've had enough rough stuff for one day,' she said. Her fingers were on my biceps and I felt compelled by manhood to tense it into a ball. She smiled. 'You're a strong boy, Eamonn, but that's the kind of strength that's only fit for knocking tree-trunks about.' She sat on the side of the bed and stretched out her hands.

'See me, I'm as weak as a kitten, but I get by. Except for that dreadful elm.' The thought of the elm made her forget her immediate predicament. We were living in a Georgian wreck, and had only one bathroom, yet we were as rich as any in the county. She couldn't invite friends. Oil was the answer not the damn Rayburn. And we should have nice taps. They didn't have to be gold-plated.

People say that visiting a church is a calming experience, but I might just as well have gone to a graveyard. I called into Joe Hassett. I said I wanted to discuss something with him. He had an office full of pretty secretaries who had picked up his language of wink and nudge. He was convinced I was after one of the girls.

'Who do you want, Deirdre or Mary?'

Their titters and his winks were too much for me, so I left.

I went up to the Grove Hotel. Rodney Barcastle spent a lot of time there. He didn't see me as I stood at the bar. I called for a Harp and smoked a Carroll's, blowing the smoke at the lifeboat. I put lime in the lager to make it more palatable. I put my back up against the bar and my shoe on the brass rail.

'Hallo, Rodney,' I said.

He glanced about before he saw me.

'Aha, the very man himself,' he said.

He was talking quietly to a group around the fire. I blew smoke at the chandelier and watched the smoke curl around the icicles. After a while I said, 'How's it going, Rodney?'

He looked up and smiled. 'Fine, lad, and yourself?'

'Great,' I said.

Then he winked a couple of times and went back to his conversation. He's a nice fellow, Rodney, a great friend of the family and especially of my mother. But this parish is filling up with winkers.

She brought me for a spin across the Golden Vale instead of going to the Grove; drink and drinkers were wearisome, she said. I will always remember the sunlit fields, the purr of the engine, and a polished red fingernail that tapped the wheel from time to time.

'I am very concerned, Eamonn,' she said, 'I'm afraid drink is going to be the death of your father.'

'The bridge?'

'No, smothering. He almost smothered last night. He twists and turns until he wraps the sheet around his head. Purple in the face he was.' That wasn't all: he had got sick in the bed, yes, and he had threatened to kill her. And me, also.

'Jesus Christ, me, too?'

'Mind your language.'

'He's going to kill us both, and you're worried about my language! If there's any killing to be done, I'll do it.'

She drew up the car and switched off. She was almost ashamed to hear her own son talk like that, and hoped that she would never again hear me say the word kill. She wanted to relax. Did I have any relaxing conversation? I fumbled through an angry mind for soothing words but gave up. I had had enough.

That night my father was banished from the bedroom to the library sofa. I couldn't sleep after the row. The ashtray beside my bed filled up with butts. Hours later I went to the loo and glanced into the library. There he was, half choking. I loosened the blankets from around his drunken head. I gazed down at the innocence of a sleeping face and it occurred to me how trusting and how vulnerable we are in that state – like children. Despite the beery smell, the wrinkles, the grey, and two-day stubble, the face of the child he once was reflected up at me as from a deep well.

My father kept a Kerry Hobby, a pet pony, that roamed the farm at will. I hid him up on the heath. My father took a bridle and we walked the farm together looking for him. I wanted to get him away from the house to confront him. He always walked in front of me. He spoke about every stone and ditch and was very proud of the way he had built up the farm. He had done all of this in just my lifetime, he said. He had married my mother when she was seventeen. He had been twenty years her senior.

'The Hobby is up on the heath, Dad, I hid him there.'

That stopped him dead in his tracks. He turned slowly.

'Yes?' he said.

I had a little speech prepared, but my mouth dried up. Little candles began to light in his eyes.

'You're giving Mum a rough time. I want it to stop.' I blurted the words out.

He looked at me for a long time, then in two quick strides he was towering over me. 'How dare you speak to me like that. How dare you interfere.'

I gritted my teeth and looked up at him, I needed aggression badly, I prayed for it but it had turned tail. My scrotum tightened almost to vanishing point. I felt my honour was about to disintegrate. Any moment my teeth would begin to chatter. In a die-hard attempt to save the situation I blurted out: 'It's a cowardly thing to hit a woman.' I didn't have time to reflect on whether it was an idiotic thing to say or not because he brought the bridle and reins, metal rings and buckles crashing down on the bridge of my nose and again across the face. He flung the bridle at my feet and with hate in his eyes stormed off. I was shocked, but not by the blows. I was shocked at the lack of anger I felt, shocked at the unmanning fear and self-pity that grabbed me by the loins. I tasted salty blood in my mouth and the tears in my eyes bent the trees and my father's stalking figure out of shape. I did not go home. Instead I found myself in the willow copse above the house, where I used to lurk as a child. I stayed there all day watching the clouds come and go, and praying for anger.

Towards evening I wandered in home. I told my mother, rather sheepishly, that I had fallen. She bathed my nose and lips by the Rayburn. 'There must be an end to falling in this house,' she hissed. I spent the night by the fire gaining some comfort from the heat and the big grandfather that ticked away the last minutes of my father's life.

At eleven-thirty I stood at the shaky bridge, my hands resting on the bolt that would plunge it into the dark powerful waters at my feet. I heard him sing in the distance as faint as my own heart-beat. I stood transfixed as the volume swelled until I could make out the words and in a trance I watched his stature grow in the moonlight. Suddenly he was striding across the bridge, my hand tightening on the bolt that fastened him to the good life. Halfway across he faltered. In that split second I thought of my mother, of the bridge, of the hate in his eyes. But to no avail. He lurched past me into the night and once again I was to know the smell of cowardice. In frustration I pulled the bolt and let the bridge crash into the stream and watched as it was dragged to the opposite bank. Then I went home and went to bed without even putting on the light.

I became obsessed with the technology of death, electricity, gas, paraquat, even the old well. Christ, the well nearly ended my life. We had it covered years ago. I managed to cut away the joists leaving only the rotten planks on top; on these I placed the Hobby's bridle hoping that Dad would fall through. He didn't, I did. But the bridle held on to something. I hung for twenty minutes over a hundred foot drop, screaming, praying, cursing. Joe Hassett of all people found me. He took me immediately to Downey's. After one pint of stout I became normal and confused, after two I felt I liked the world, after three I was master of Earth, at the fourth I got sick all over Downey's floor and was thrown out. I got sick in the kitchen and my mother screamed at Joe all the way to his Granada. As waves of nausea began to blacken out my mind that night, I knew I had no stomach for murder.

I cut my father out of my heart. He began to spend his nights in the old dairy. There were no more rows. I heard my mother mutter about social withdrawal and insanity. I used to happen upon him in the empty barn sitting on a ladder and sighing to himself. I was totally indifferent, and proud of it.

I came home from school at a clip, threw the Yamaha up against the wall, and stormed into the kitchen. I banged my books on the table and called for my mother. She called me up to her room. I raced up the stairs and entered her room and then stopped short. My mother was sitting at the dressing-table combing her hair with not a stitch of clothes on save for a small black skirt. I wheeled to run, but she called me back and made me sit on the bed. Her long blonde hair streamed down between her breasts which swayed slightly as she chose a clip and deftly fastened a lock of gold. Her blue eyes never glanced once at me, she just continued to comb. My embarrassment drained away and suddenly knew that this situation was the most natural thing in the world. She was thirty-five, but could pass for twenty-five, and her breasts hadn't the slightest trace of chins.

'Another half-day?'

She lisped the words because her lips held two clips. Suddenly the memory of school came back and I blurted out how Mr Burke had thrown me out of Honours Science because of all the absences. He had called me a pup. I called him a drunkard. Everybody is a drunkard in this fucking country, if you ask me. I beat the bed with my fists and screamed that I'd kill Mr Burke. She took a clip from her mouth and secreted it in the toss of gold. She squinted coyly at the mirror to see if it suited. It did.

'I've had enough,' I screamed.

'School?'

'Yes.'

'Well, it's about time you gave it up.'

I looked at her in amazement.

'You mean I can give it up?'

'Yes,' she said.

It was a strange world, she said, when the deprived, like Mr Burke, could tell the likes of me what life was about. Then she suddenly got up and took me by the hand and led me to the window.

'Look out there,' she said. 'What do you see? You see thousands of acres of prime land, three hundred and fourteen of woodland, one hundred and eighty-eight acres of lake, bog and moor, three sand-pits, one limestone quarry, hunting, shooting and fishing rights, one Georgian manor and four cottages to house our workers, and not one penny in income tax. Will your sonnets put gas in the Volvo? Will chemistry feed the bullocks? Can Rodney Barcastle remember the title of a Shakespeare play? I could bet Joe Hassett one of his combine harvesters that he hasn't got a sentence of Irish in his head. The world is upside down, but it's all yours.' And she embraced me. I didn't know what to do with my hands. She went back to the dressing-table and put on a black bra, then a gold chain with one diamond around her neck. 'Which reminds me, isn't it time you met some nice girls?'

'But I already have a girl, Mom, Debbie.'

'Debbie?' She said the name a few times to herself, moistening her lips with her tongue.

I thought of Debbie peering at me over the chessboard. I thought about her with this new confidence, with new insight into my own importance and I knew that if I was to be master of an upside-down world, Debbie would not do. I discovered a calm indifference.

'O.K., Mom, I agree.'

'How about a nice girl like Jean O'Reilly?' She glanced coyly at me and must have seen that the name struck home. I gasped at the thought of Jean's face. How often had her indifferent glance at me made me quail. My mother put on her blouse, got up and patted me on the back.

'Leave Jean O'Reilly to me,' she said. 'Now take the dog for a walk before dinner.'

I walked in triumph through the farm admiring the green saviours of my life.

The sledge-hammer was driving a wedge. The sound carried deep and slow on the cold air. I made my way to the top of a hill where a fine stand of elm had taken the disease. He had just trimmed one trunk which he had half split. Power and tension radiated from the opening cleft. I could almost feel the wedges vibrate, their thick ends almost level with the bark. I placed his tea on the ground and walked over to hand him the cigarettes my mother had bought for him. Neither of us looked the other in the eye and that's why we dropped them between us into the cleft. Instinctively he reached after them and that he should not have done. The trunk closed like a door on his hand, the wedges shot off like bullets. I heard the timber crush his hand like eggshell and at the same time his screams. His screams scared the hell out of me. I tried to pull his hand out, but he just fell unconscious on top of the log. The last shred of sense deserted me and all I could do was shout for help. It was useless, our farm was much too big. I couldn't find the wedges so I headed home downhill at a gallop. I ran into the yard shouting like mad, but nobody was there, the Volvo was gone, the labourers had gone. I tore the Yamaha out of the shed and leapt on the kick-starter. At that moment I glanced up at the wood on the hill and thought of my father's bare back on the log. Night and cold were slithering down the mountain fast towards him. I gunned the bike out onto the road and sped west, slicing the evening in two. I felt its power surge through my body as I passed Gleeson's gate, then O'Hanrahan's, then McCarthy's. I didn't have either leathers or helmet and I didn't care. On through Skreen, Rathmichael, Killmorna at full throttle. At the ruined water-mill in Templebeg I ran out of petrol. As I walked home the clouds were rolled back and whatever heat was in the earth rose towards the stars. I slept so soundly that my mother had to shake me.

'Where's your father? He didn't come home last night.'

'Better try the Flesk, he must have gone to Downey's last night.'

When I came back from the river the Gardaí and some neighbours were in the yard.

'You brought him tea on the hill yesterday evening?' said the sergeant.

'Yes, sir.'

'And he wasn't in Downey's last night. We'll have to try the last place he was seen then.'

We trudged up through the wood.

The thing about people who die outdoors is that their eyes remain open. My father's looked into the very narrow split in the timber as if in his last moments he had reproved the thing he loved so much. I noticed that and his boots. Some of the studs on the soles were almost worn. The sight of these studs, in some strange way, moved me to some compassion. I was thankful for such an honest human emotion. I heard the sledge drive the wedge and I felt the deep shivering of the timber in my heart. Somebody caught me by the waist just as I fell and put me sitting on the log. A bottle was put to my lips and I tasted some sort of whiskey.

The Gardaí and neighbours brought him down. Joe Hassett took me by the arm and led me all the way to the house. He remained sort of close to me until the day of the funeral. All I can remember of that day is Rodney Barcastle accompanying my mother from the cemetery.

It became more convenient for me to cook my own food, seeing all the trouble that was caused by the alterations. There were fellows in there knocking down walls; pipes and wires and paint were all over the house. My mother was a little overpowered by it all and I was glad to help. What with all the sympathisers coming and going and the inquest, she had gone through a lot. Sometimes I used to wait up for her at night, or maybe stroll down for a game of chess to Debbie's. But my mother was right. I couldn't see an awful lot in Debbie any more.

One night mother and I sat by the fire in the drawing-room. There were lots of magazines lying about on fashion, clothes, and colour schemes for walls. I was just about to discuss the possibility of our going to Dublin for the Spring Show when she spoke without looking up from her magazine.

'Why didn't your father drink his tea?'

The question nearly knocked me out of the chair. Those events had gone cold in my mind. She asked the question a second time. This time the nonchalance was punctuated by the turning of pages.

'I don't know,' I said.

'It came back frozen in the flask with not a drop taken from it. Your father was so thirsty from Downey's the night before, he should have drunk it at one gulp. What happened when you gave him the tea?'

'I don't know, I can't remember.'

'And the cigarettes. How did they get into the split? And the box was unopened. What I'd like to know is when did all of this happen?'

'Goodness, Mom, I haven't an – '

'Answer me,' she cut in on me.

'I don't know, Mom.' I was hurt and I was scared. 'The inquest cleared all that up, it was due to exposure. Why are you raking over that now?' I must have bleated.

She got up and arranged the magazines neatly on the table.

'You are just like your father, Eamonn, thick.'

I felt the old feeling of being drained in the pit of my stomach, a lack of aggression, the smell of defeat. There was malice i‹ her words and I felt the metal rings on the bridge of my nose again. She walked gracefully across the room and paused at the door with her hand on the knob.

'Where the tree is felled is where you find the chippings.'

There was mockery in the words. My thoughts floundered as I searched for an answer but she had gone quietly, closing the hall door ever so gently. Shortly after the Volvo slid down the drive. It was the first time my mother had repeated one of my father's proverbs. She always hated them because they belonged to the old world. When she used ask my father why he was always chopping wood instead of burning oil, he used to say, 'He who chops his own wood burns it twice.'

It used to infuriate her.

I can't remember whether it was the sound of the central heating system or the voices which wakened me, but I was drenched in sweat and decided to cool off. Then I decided to investigate the voices which were coming from my mother's room. There was a big hole in the wall left by the heating engineers which they had yet to fill. There was a night light beside my mother's bed. Joe Hassett had just made love to my mother, their limbs sprawled all over each other, Joe gasping, last year's sun still on my mother's body. Her hair sprawled all over the pillow. There was a certain calm, a familiarity with each other which told me this was not the first time. I didn't mind. If it made my mother happy, that was fine with me. I spent ages watching and listening to my heart beat. Suddenly my mother spoke.

'Joe.'

'Yeah?'

'Joe, I think he's going to kill himself.'

'How?'

'I don't know, maybe on that motorbike of his.'

Joe didn't answer. I couldn't read his features, but I could see the pupil of his eye glittering in the night light. It looked to me as evil as the well I almost fell through. I tried to sound the world at that moment, but I couldn't strike bottom. I detached myself from the scene, backing slowly down the stairs. I felt I had been struck by a heavy blow on the head, I felt so dull and stupid. But fear began to take control and I quickly gathered my things. I crept quietly down to the old dairy. There were three locks on it, he knew what he was doing. Between the fear and the disaster there is great illumination and I felt my head fill with light.

Inside there were siege measures everywhere, no piped water, no gas, no electricity. All food in cans or dried. Nothing could be tampered with. I lit a storm lamp and saw my shadow huge against the gable wall.

There was a note on the table.

'Shotgun and cartridges in false architrave of door.'

I checked. It was there, gleaming and polished. I sat down on the bed and my mind began to clear slowly as if the hiss of the storm lantern had power to drive away the mist that befogged my head. Who was the note for? I had a very funny feeling and I looked about the dairy, my eyes peering among the long shadows. I felt I was not alone any more. Once my father had said that there were three kinds of people: one the hammer, two the wedge, three the split wood. Wedge I had been, split wood I now was. Could I ever be the hammer?

The way I figure things is this: life is like a tragic drama on television. There are two ways to play it, backwards or forwards. I prefer backwards because that way you always finish with a happy beginning.

The Banquet of Life

Brother Xavier was very tall and was always afraid of being struck by lightning. He was worn out from listening for thunderclaps and keeping an eye out for black clouds, especially on humid summer days, which were very dangerous, he said. On a very cold day he met Brother Fergus outside the orchard gate. Fergus was remarkable for nothing other than the way one forgot him so easily, only to remember him suddenly at some extraordinary time for no reason at all. Fergus suspected this and was satisfied, for it was the way he and the monkish rule designed it: to be outstanding at nothing other than the keeping of his vows of chastity, poverty and obedience. As Xavier was much older, Fergus made an overture to the age gap.

'Cold weather these days, Xavier, almost as bad as '44.'

'No, no. 1944 wasn't cold at all. That was '41, fright to God with snow.'

'Then what happened in '44?'

'1944 was terrible for 'flu, dying in the ditches they were.'

'I thought that was '47?'

'Nothing happened in '47.' He raised his wet eyes, looking southward over the monastery wall, and said with finality, 'No, Brother, '47 was no class of a year at all.'

Xavier was also a part-time gardener and when Fergus inquired whether he was going to do some digging he replied no, now that Celestius had died, he had been appointed Bursar and was too busy. Fergus congratulated him and hurried to his cell where he threw himself on his bed in despair.

He had always wanted to be Bursar, not for the little power that went with it but for the delight it would give him to see the monastery prosper. For the Little Brothers of the Cross were in the red.

Already Finbarr, the Superior, gave long talks after Little Office about unnecessary bus journeys, while at meals those passages from Rodriguez which urged fasting and self-mortification were most commonly heard.

It was his custom when frightened to lie still on his bed and ease the thwarted passion of his heart by thinking of all the good things that had ever happened to him. Not least of these was the decision which had anchored him to his present way of life. He had become a monk not because he thought the world needed reforming but because it was good and should stay that way. His decision hadn't gone unobserved by the begrudgers: 'Why only a Brother? Why can't he become a priest and be closer to God?' But Fergus was humble. Not that he hadn't considered all the other choices: Mr Fergus, Dr Fergus, Fr Fergus, Br Fergus. They all had an 'R' in common, he had told himself with a smile.

He had refused a position in a local bank, which puzzled both his friends and himself. For in his own parish he was regarded as a wizard with figures and an astute judge of the price of everything from in-calf heifers to second-hand bicycles. However, his father wouldn't let him sell cattle at the fair because he had a terrible fault, he was honest. He wasn't at all worldly. As he had said to Brother Eamonn, 'Eamonn, before I became a monk I had a German shotgun, a red setter and a tweed top-coat that was as warm as thatch. I gave them all away to my Uncle Dinny.' Eamonn made no comment but he was very impressed, for he himself had been in short pants when he entered the novitiate.

Fergus felt better already. He got off the bed and stretched himself. He looked around at the bare white walls of his cell, the bed with its starched sheets, the chair, the little window, curtainless because monks have nothing to hide, and the simple deal table on which lay the *Little Office of the Virgin Mary*. These were all tangible things that gave him confidence because he knew his exact relationship to them. He looked down at the shining parquet floor and filled his lungs with the antiseptic smell of polish. It was the smell of the monkish life, for him the smell of home.

A few days later, Finbarr, the Superior, called Fergus to his office. Finbarr was a returned missionary from some steamy jungle and as a result was given to mild swearing, gin and bitters and sweating at the oddest of times. He was an avowed enemy of General Okchumbo, who had burned the mission school, raped the Little Sisters of Kilkenny, and sent the pupils back to the jungle after they had been made burn their Clery's underwear. He was also very short with monks who had not been abroad.

'Dear Brother,' he said, choosing the formal address, 'now that Celestius has left us you will be taking the scholarship class for Latin, Irish, English, History, Geography and, of course, the usual Christian Doctrine. Have you any comment?'

'Yes. Is there anything else?'

'Yes, Accountancy or Drawing as an extra.'

Fergus went down the steps to the school with a heavy heart despite the sweetener of Accountancy. As he walked across the school yard he happened to meet Jack MacCarthy. The relationship between monk and layman on the staff was good but remote at the best of times; Fergus was an exception to many rules. He looked at the pale face and tired eyes. 'Goodness, where were you last night?'

'A reunion, Brother, old friends, a few pints.'

'Why don't you drink half pints and save twice as much?'

Jack said that it was a great idea, that he hadn't thought of it before.

That night Fergus's chest felt very heavy as he lay on his bed. It wasn't rebellion at the scholarship class, he told himself, for he believed in the motto: 'To toil and not to seek for rest, to labour and to look for no reward.' Absolute obedience kept the soul from 'getting notions', as the Master of Novices had confided to him once. And in the Novitiate he had been tested and not found wanting. Six times he'd taken his meals on his knees; often he scrubbed the same kitchen floor more than twice in the one day, and now and again throwing in a piece of the hall to show there was no rancour. Sacrifice and its afterglow of sanctifying grace were what the monastic rule was all about.

The rhythm of the school timetable and the canonical hours farmed a tidy routine out of his day; it relieved him of the responsibility of choice; it offered the opportunity for self-mortification which would scour the soul of hurt and resentment. And when those doubts that prey upon resolve floated all the way up to his head he sank them with salvoes of work and vow. Both he and the pupils relished the accountancy classes, he making millions for them in stocks and shares, they spending with tight budgets.

One day in the corridor he met a very angry Jack MacCarthy, who waved a slip of paper over his head, saying Jesus, what was he going to do with only a hundred, and Christmas on top of him. Fergus took it out of his hand and looked for the first time at a Departmental pay cheque. It was a jam of figures, allowances, rebates, responsibility payments. The excitement of coming face to face with an alien world only lasted a moment before Jack retrieved his slip and went muttering upon his way. Fergus was left standing alone in the corridor, his fingers tingling.

They still tingled that night as he sat looking through the white walls of his cell. It had never occurred to him that there was such a thing as money involved in the work he did. Of course the Bursar got Fergus's money and that went to pay for the missions abroad. That was the real difference between himself and Jack MacCarthy. That finding gave him a certain satisfaction and he smiled.

A few days later he got a reply to his discreet inquiry from the Department of Education. They said he was earning £2,500. He threw the letter on the table, paced the floor and said it couldn't be right. In the last twenty years he had never handled more than a bus fare. Eamonn couldn't manage the immensity either. He scratched his grey hair and said that he remembered when for ten bob you could get a secondhand pellet gun, a bundle of American comics and a big bag of sweets.

Immediately after vespers a week later Fergus took down a ledger. Then, wrestling with a few dark doubts, he entered his name, address, registration number and neatly, in a column opposite, £2,500. He felt like a piece of silver that had just been stamped in the assayer's office. His exhilaration was not born out of avarice. He told himself there was no point in making a sacrifice unless one knew the exact extent of it. He gazed in admiration at the pound symbol. It had a devilish design like a graceful dancing foot that tapped out old forgotten rhythms. But they were rhythms best forgotten he told himself, and for many a day afterwards the figures on the open page summoned him at extraordinary times to bear witness to the greed of man. He would stand above the green-lined page and listen to the distant traffic: was it for this that streams of hooting steel ground through the city? For such a paltry thing as this the hurly-burly of man would go on? Eamonn didn't like money either. 'I hate round things like balls, rings and shillings. Give me cornery things any day like doors, fields and the pages of a book.'

One day after compline, Fergus discreetly took the letter he had got from the Inland Revenue to his cell and opened it. For the first time in his life he experienced the resentment and helplessness of a man who was being legally cheated. When he deducted £500 he still had £2000, all his own; he whispered the sum to himself as he would some pious aspiration, and as he felt again the mounting triumph within him he paused to think of home. Home was an enchantment that the lean years had exorcised, leaving only a few scattered moments to the memory; the tramp of hobnailed boots along the quay wall, sad mackerel eyes drying in the sun, and whistles chasing dogs in the hills above the cliffs; and Mom and Dad. He would never forget her that day at the station at the edge of a little knot of friends. She dried her eyes, the engines hooted, she waved her handkerchief as the train moved off and a light went out of her life for ever. They came awkwardly to the city for his profession. His father had been very impressed by the luxury of the Head House and the quality of the soil in the extensive grounds. He was delighted also that the family now had a friend at the court of the Lord, ready to whisper in the right ear at a time of crisis.

Two hundred pounds was not too niggardly a sum to send them he hoped. This left him with £1800 all his, all debts discharged.

The presence of his accounts book in his life troubled him, but he told himself such harmless fun would keep him from getting bored. He had once known a monk who used to chew through rosary beads from boredom. He had heard him in the cell next door crack the beads like toffee balls and spit the pieces into the hand basin.

He met Jack MacCarthy at the little break and edged him away from the beaten desperate conversation of his colleagues. He asked him what an apartment was like and was told that, of course, he meant a bedsitter.

'What's the difference?'

Jack closed one eye and squinted at wisdom in the fire. 'If you tried to move all the rooms of a house into one room you'd get something close to it. I have one in Rathmines – gas ring, table, bookshelf, wardrobe, chest of drawers, press for food, double bed.'

'Why double?'

'For comfort. And posters on the wall.'

The whole thing had an ascetic leanness that Fergus approved of. He then asked Jack what he did with all his money. When Jack recovered he saw that Fergus was still quite serious. He glanced around him cautiously before answering: 'The little jar and the little woman.'

'Tobacco?'

'Rarely. Few teachers can afford all three.'

Fergus hastened away, not without a certain amount of distaste. All that money on drugs and women.

It was with thrilling expectancy that he sat down that day to anatomise £1,800 into essentials. He was going to make a lot of money because he neither drank nor smoked, and naturally women were out of the question. Well, he didn't know; he was a man after all, as he and his confessor knew too well; but he had found to his satisfaction that whispered aspirations and the caustic Latin insulted the flesh into submission. Still, he occasionally remembered Norry Mitchell. She must have been fourteen or so. Always wore blue, to go with her eyes, no doubt, and thick blond curls that crowded her forehead. She must have been a very sensitive child for she always blushed whenever they chanced to meet. Still, he would have liked to touch her golden hair, it would have been cool and silky. He would have stroked that white throat, it would have been soft, softer than anything his hand would ever touch in the monastery. He would have liked to – he took up his pen with a flourish and made an inscription, twelve pounds to the A.S.T.I., his Teachers' Union. Money down the drain but it possibly gave a sense of belonging, he hoped.

The rest was easy although he howled at the speed of his ebbing capital. Food, shoes, clothes – he bought himself a camel hair topcoat – a bedsitter in Rathmines, books and magazines for his shelves, and suitcases for going on holidays. Opposite each entry he placed his projected costs. On subtraction he was left with only £800. It was so small he gasped. He decided that in lay life each hour in the twenty-four was a mendicant whose bony hand demanded a toll before passing you by. Still he felt a certain rapture after all his hard work.

Being a businessman and a gambler, he found it difficult to allow so much money to lie fallow. He took a more serious interest in stocks and shares. He learned quickly, checking each forecast against the prices quoted each day in the newspapers, and never made the same mistake twice. Soon he had mastered the intricacies of the exchange so well that he could chase recurring decimals back two weeks from memory. He could run his eye down the wavy column of fractions as easily as he would scan a line of Virgil at school. It only took him three months to reach £1,200. He was so triumphant that he felt he had to show Eamonn; he had misgivings about that for Eamonn had a vigorous cynicism which sometimes was a force of pure negation. 'It's like me counting indulgences and sometimes cooking the books, harmless.'

Fergus didn't like metaphors, for metaphors were lies.

He refused to spend money until he knew the exact price. He sent away for cut-price lists, mail-order lists and catalogues for records, golf clubs, shotguns and Waterford glass – all the trappings of a worldly man. He didn't leave them lying around his cell but neither would he hide them for there was nothing underhand about him. He placed them tidily among his underwear in the wardrobe.

He was doing so well with Youghal Carpets, Imperial Chemicals, Irish Distillers, Katanga Copper, that he bought himself a Volks from the small ads: 1964, metallic gold, lovely condition, leopardskin seats, p.m.o. £120 o.n.o. It was a real bargain, especially the leopardskin. He deducted for everything including petrol (Regular).

The other monks, when they heard of Fergus's new hobby, gave mild approval. Every man needs something to call his own, they said, he had been looking bad lately, he was working too hard, he was no different from Brother Terence, who was interested in tropical diseases, or Peter, who was writing a thesis on '*T*' *buailte* in old Irish.

The morning newspapers were short on financial information. One morning Jack MacCarthy slipped a packet to Fergus. That evening he opened in his cell for the first time the *Financial Times*, that great record of pink greed. This was progress; he had given the pupils no homework that night, which delighted them, for their teacher had become unpredictable lately. This new source of information gave more scope to the gambler in him and as a result he climbed recklessly to the magic of £1,500. All his, not a single penny owing, and he was only thirty-five.

Jack MacCarthy continued to smuggle until one morning he came in late, looking tired, without the *Times*, and said he was getting married to a girl called Diana. He did; his health improved, and Fergus was happy for him. It was bad for a man 'outside' to be single. Eamonn, who knew a lot about Gods and Goddesses, said Diana was goddess of the hunt, and that he had seen her on a bus and she was very good-looking.

Lent came on, grey and demanding, hand in hand with cold rain, fasting and endless smoked haddock. His class of insatiable scholars sent him out one day into the city to scour the bookshops for more facts, more ways to cheat the examiners. It was late and the raucous streets struggled to cope with the violence of the homeward race. There was a slush on the ground and the lights, weak in the fog, did little for the darkness of his soul. Hordes of perished faces jostled him, each with the same fish mouth, like a school of terrified mackerel savaging each other in the net.

As he crossed O'Connell Bridge he couldn't help noticing a young woman detach herself from the tide, fumble in her purse and toss a coin to a derelict mouth-organ player who was sprawled on the footpath. Fergus, never having much more than bus fares, did not give alms. He saw her profile briefly. Shining dark hair curled in under a relaxed jaw, a moist smiling mouth and an eye so brown and beautiful that it troubled him. Just as he was about to pass, she turned and danced gracefully into the crowd in front of him. He couldn't avoid following her, for a path seemed to open magically in the throng for her. He couldn't avoid taking pleasure in her hair which danced to the rhythm of her walk as did her mini-skirt which swayed high above her knees. His eyes admiringly traced the elegant lines that curved from sweet thigh down to firm ankle.

Yet he told himself that it wasn't the swaying body nor the face with all its beauty that attracted him, but the promise in her mouth. The only mouth that smiled at a beggar in months. He would give a lot to see that smile again. It was easily worth twenty shares in Gulf Oil.

But the racing of his blood was being balanced by a familiar depression. The girl was simply too beautiful for words. A girl like this could have any man she wished. She paused to buy a paper at Trinity College and Fergus had to do likewise. 'Th-th-th-the Evening P-P-P-Press,' she said, and Fergus was startled out of his wits. He followed her at a safe distance up Dawson Street, saying delightedly to himself 'Evening P-P-P-ress.' He was sure he loved girls with stutters. Eamonn had told him that Japanese potters always put an artificial blemish in too perfect a vase. It was so right. Down Baggot Street they went and Fergus's heart pumped for love and pity. Pity because not many men would like a stutter. A faint breeze gave him a whiff of perfume and he felt weak. But there was no question of his stopping, for he was no longer in command. Some devilish energy propelled his limbs, and locked the senses of his body to the sensual rhythm ahead. He passed the bookshop and didn't give a damn.

She mounted granite steps to a Georgian door. As she paused to fumble for her keys she looked nonchalantly down at the passing cleric. Their eyes met for a moment as brief as the rustle of silk, but to him there was a whole eternity in it. Then she was gone and the bang of the door echoed all over the street, leaving him alone with strangers. And the echo said in a deep voice: 'Brother Fergus, you are outlawed from the Banquet of Life and shall always be thus.' He had never stopped for one minute, but now his feet seemed to weigh tons and the effort made him gulp in lungfuls of polluted Dublin air. Suddenly he remembered to blow on his fingers against the cold. Even though he was going in the wrong direction, he continued down Baggot Street and every head of black hair he saw he thought he recognised it. His heart was trying to run away with him some place. Baggot Street was strange territory with its tall buildings full to the eaves with flats. Already doors were banging all over the street and lights were shining through curtains – red, blue, yellow; happy lights, happy people, he hoped. He rested his arms on Baggot Street Bridge and looked into the black canal waters. From the depths came brown eyes and a smile that chilled his blood. He had spent his bus fare on the *Evening Press*. passers-by eyed suspiciously the figure in clerical garb that sprawled on the bridge wall.

Next morning Fergus listened to Eamonn discourse on Irish Goddesses Morioghan, Brighid, Dana, Cliodhna. And what was

Dana the Goddess of? Of the Earth, he believed. Terence, the Infirmarian, who doubled as quack psychologist, was consulted on stutters. Stutters were curable and never as bad as a squint. One had to wait for a cure however, for they came and went as they pleased, like warts and mushrooms. They might be connected with bad habits although afflicted people usually had the grace of God.

And so she came to grow on Fergus as easy as a wild flower in the forest, Dana, the goddess of the earth. Matins, nones, lauds, vespers – each canonical hour marked a stage in her reconstruction. 'Nunc dimmittis servum tuum,' his voice would roll forth the Latin as confidently as any of his colleagues. He noticed for the first time that they all had kind faces but were a little unhappy. It was his duty to liven them up a little and so Fergus became very chatty and full of earnest advice.

Magazines such as *Vogue* and *Woman's Way* began to appear in his wardrobe. Little deductions were made in his accounts book for chocolates and handkerchiefs. He became more aware of colour and decided the monastery was very dull. He placed flowers in his cell.

At the end of the week the monthly session of redition took place. It was a public confession by each monk including the risk of being accused by others. Only the old monks took it seriously. Peter accused Jeremiah of banging pots and pans unnecessarily in the kitchen, Terence was accused of making too free with the monastery dog. But when Xavier in a stentorian voice accused Fergus of keeping daffodils in his cell there was silence. In a faltering voice he had begged their forgiveness. 'I am heartily sorry, Brethren, and I request a penance of your own very dear Brother.' He gave back the flowers and said five full Rosaries. Nobody had ever accused him of anything in his life before. It confused him and brought him to the verge of tears.

He got no more copies of the *Financial Times*. He felt that Jack MacCarthy wanted to avoid him. One evening he sat looking at the only one he had left. He picked out shares at 2/6d in an exploration company in Australia called Poseidon. He asked Eamonn. 'Oh yes, Poseidon was a Greek God of the sea, I believe.' He was becoming involved in the whole pantheon. He felt a little crazy buying £1,000 worth, but then he was beleagured.

He immersed himself even more in his magazines. One day he walked all round the monastery looking for someone who could explain to him what taffeta was. He had paused outside Eamonn's door but he felt that Eamonn did not want to be bothered. He went back to his cell and read the horoscopes. They told him that it was fatal for Virgo to dither that week. That is why he married Dana on the 15th, his feast day; not without having a good look at his accounts. But the women's magazines had said any old wedding would cost £300. He bit his lip at the cost but it was worth it for a goddess. She was from Oughterard, where her father kept a pub and did very well. He was a small jolly man who was quick to pull a pint for weary travellers; of course he didn't drink at all himself; and he liked Fergus. Her mother was even nicer and was much given to gingerbread recipes. It was a great day and Fergus paid for the reception. The magazines had neglected to mention that her father would have wanted to do that. All the local luminaries were there – the Parish Priest and the Sergeant, who was a great friend of the family. Uncle Dinny was Fergus's best man; he still wore Fergus's top coat, he was pleased to see.

For the honeymoon they went to Spain, which is a very hot country, and Fergus bought himself sunglasses. It was also fortunate that he had previously invested in suitcases. They came home very tanned and added the room next door to their bedsitter, leaving them an apartment. Fergus had to cobble the books in earnest in order to keep up such a high standard of living.

The canonical hours chimed by, punctuating his bliss. He chanted the office and sang psalms with the verve of a man with a purpose. And while he worked hard at his job, he couldn't help thinking of Dana all on her own in the flat. She must have been lonely, he thought, and he would have to think of something.

Towards term's end Jack MacCarthy came into the school one morning looking ill and announced that he was the father of a daughter. Fergus almost kicked himself when he heard it. He went straight to his cell and gave birth to a baby boy, one up on Jack. it was a terrible cost – £200 in a private nursing home, but they were worth it – the pair of them.

There were three of them, Dana, Fergus and Fergusheen. But something had to be done. He wasn't satisfied to see his family in a tenement. Rathmines was a slum, so was Rathgar, and Dublin wasn't a whole lot better. He would build a big house just outside the city with a conservatory and big garden. She would love the conservatory and spend the morning there pruning roses; and the country air would be good for Fergusheen's health.

But he hadn't a penny left. It was all tied up in Poseidon shares. He sneaked into town one afternoon and bought the *Financial Times*. He took a look at it and staggered all the way back to the monastery. He took it to the bathroom and looked at it once more. Poseidon had gone from 2/6d to £143. That couldn't be right, things like that didn't happen. if it were true he was worth £1,144,000. Was he suffering from delusions? No, but it was better to check.

Next day he asked Jack MacCarthy to bring in the *Times* again. Fergus was delighted when he said he would. Jack wondered why Fergus had decided to speak to him again.

That night he slept fitfully, turning and turning in the white stiff sheets, waking in confusion only to be slowly reminded of where he was by the soft ticking of his travelling clock. The early classes next morning were fragile things. He made mistakes in Latin and was quite sharp with his pupils at Christian Doctrine.

A few minutes before little break Fergus made his way across the yard to the lay staff-room. As the teachers came in one by one they stared at the pale red-eyed cleric who stood to attention in the middle of the room. The only sound to be heard was the fumbling at the primus stove. When Jack MacCarthy came in Fergus tore the *Times* out of his hand and buried his eyes in the middle of it.

'Jesus Christ,' he said in a peculiar voice, 'I've made seven thousand pounds in twenty-four hours.' He stalked out of the room and across the yard. The *Financial Times* dropped from his hands. The wind leafed through its pages and blew them high over the school buildings, where like crazy pink seagulls they tumbled in a grey sky.

It was with great determination and a light sweat on his forehead that Fergus entered Finbarr's office without knocking and explained that for the first time he was in a position to help the monastery, that his wife and kid wouldn't need all the £1,151,000, and that there was no more to worry about.

Finbarr said that was great news and engaged Fergus in animated conversation as he brought him down to the east wing where there were very nice rooms with a southern aspect on the garden.

The bars neatly sliced the sunlight, throwing their net on the polish of the infirmary floor. Outside all was quiet, apologetic.

Fergus lay buried in the sheets. Only his glasses, his nose and some steam were visible. Xavier slouched in, smelling of earth and grass-cutting. He carried a large bunch of flowers. When he spoke, his voice seemed to come all the way up from his boots.

'Woodbine, fairyfingers, dandelion, dogrose and ragwort, a true litany of weeds, don't you think?' He placed them on the bedside locker. 'On the other hand, what are weeds but flowers that have poor public relations?' His deep laughter made his massive frame shake, which in turn shook the room. He pulled two apples out from somewhere, rubbed them on his soutane, and offered one to Fergus. 'Cox's orange pippins, we'll have a little treat.' He sat on the edge of the bed and all the springs groaned under him. There was a snap of an apple being bitten. 'I'll be needing some help in the garden for a while. It would do us both good.' Fergus said he would.

When he went, Finbarr entered, with a laundry bag full of accountancy books and magazines. 'I cleaned your room for you,' he said. Fergus never having been on the missions, Finbarr had little else to say to him. As he left he advised him to pray to the Holy Ghost.

Peter, who was in charge of supplies, came in after Little Office. He was always shy and remote and usually struggled in company. He stood in the middle of the floor. His father had been a shoemaker, a fact that made him respectful of footwear. He suddenly pulled Fergus's big rubber shoes from under the bed and said, 'I'll get you shoes, dear Brother, real leather ones.'

Fergus opened the door of the infirmary. It was almost dark. He looked up the passage. It was a long passage that lost itself in gloom. His shoes creaked as he walked slowly down. In the distance he could hear the Latin being sung. They were singing for gods and maybe for goddesses. Outside, fog from the city spilled in over the monastery walls. He tightened his scarf for it would freeze tonight.

The Atheist

The day after she was buried the cork blew off her elderberry wine. It was only then he knew she was dead and that he would never see her again. The bird had not flown. She hadn't even been snatched. She had been torn through the bars of the cage, leaving some blood and a fine down lingering in the air. It was this fine down that drifted through his mind now, eternally heavy, deathlessly cold. He stood in a bay window somewhere on planet earth, which was but a stone twirling in the sunbeams, and he wanted to shout out her name loud enough for it to ring out for all time, he wanted the whole universe to know how much he loved her. But he didn't. For he knew he might as well talk to a rocking horse. He watched the curtains being sucked out into the garden by the gale. He looked up at the sky. Nothing except cloud chasing cloud, and somewhere above them the moon and all the stars. All dead. There were no other worlds. There were no more dimensions. There was merely what is. No could be's, should be's, might be's, maybe's. Just the reality of the indicative, and the nightmare of subjunctives. There was merely Time and if you were in it, you were of it. And at any given time there was only one micro second and we were all, all five billion of us, biting on it together. And as we bit, each one of us journeyed towards our eternity and the road flying from under us.

He cursed intelligence, culture, education and insight. These things had deprived him of the comfort of a God, and the solace of a happy eternity united with loved ones. But in a way he was proud that he felt like this, for such loneliness was dearly bought and paid for in Ireland. She would have felt the same if it had been he who had died, for she too was a lonely disbeliever.

He had envied the others at the graveside, the weeping relatives and friends, as the sods thumped down on her coffin. Their show of emotion went with their religion. He remained erect, whitefaced, and fierce throughout it all. Dry-eyed atheism. If she could hear he would beg her forgiveness for the awful funeral and tell her that it wasn't his fault. They, that is both his and her relatives, wouldn't hear of cremation. Her brothers would attack him. It was taken out of his hands and was a traditional funeral: priests, splashing of holy water, full requiem mass. Some woman sang *Lacrimosa Dies Illa*, she would have liked that. But the rest of it was sordid, and the display of religiosity and piety especially from her side of the family was sickening. How had so fine a mind as hers escaped from that dunghill called the extended family? Yes, forgive him all the bowing and scraping. For the last few days he was as a man tumbling through another's dream. But what was the point in talking to her, for he knew that a few seconds after the head-on collision on the Killshaskin Road the billion, billion cells of information that was Emer de Brun, flickered out one by one, all the poetry, laughter, plans, music, memories of her father, taste of blackberries, smell of fuchsia in the Gaeltacht, joy of dawn, the know-how for making plum puddings stay alight, the feeling of cool windowpanes with the rain streaming on the outside, the warmth of a kiss from the man she loved – all gone like the snows of yesteryear. And he had paid the priest. It was ironic that the only contact she ever had with priests since she became an independent teenager was at her death. Fr O'Herlihy had gently suggested that now he might reconsider his ways and start coming to church. He gave him a most emphatic no. As she would have done. It was a bitter cross to carry – to carry in Ireland – the cross of Godlessness. But carry it he would through dungeon, fire and sword.

Suddenly the movement in the scullery brought him back to reality. The symphony of rattles, bangings, tinklings, rubbings, scrapings, and poundings that was titled 'Life must go on' carried all over the house. Then silence. Then the footsteps of Julia, her mother, slow and heavy up the hallway, then the pause, then the rattle, the knob and the creak of the door. He didn't turn but he felt eyes peering at him, as if someone had parted the curtains in another world and gazed at the miracle of a man standing alone in his own bay window.

'You can't go on like this.' The voice was taut but quiet, telling of the effort of resignation. 'You'll have to eat, even a little.'

He didn't turn, nor did he reply. He felt totally indifferent to her and to his own bad manners. She coughed, then paused before saying: 'If you don't eat we'll be running another body into the ground. 'Tis what she would have liked – that you should eat something, even a small bit.' She was only here a few days he thought and already she knew that to mention her was the way to get him to act. He teetered for a moment then sighed and turned and said almost inaudibly: 'Whatever you say.' They went to the kitchen. The meal she had prepared was prawn provencale. It had always been their favourite meal together. Now, to eat it without her seemed thoughtless. He would have preferred something more neutral like a hamburger. He ate a forkful and nibbled at a piece of bread. She sat opposite him and watched him eat. Then as if she felt it was the right time she said quietly: 'I know how you feel about the mass cards. It is a pity, but that's the way it is. Remember it's love and sorrow that makes people go to pay a priest for a mass card. You'll have to read them, there are 220 in all. They are mostly from people who couldn't attend the funeral. They will have to be answered. I've a list of the people who sent wreaths. They must all be acknowledged.' He went on chewing. He found himself wondering why they had been so attracted to each other. It had he thought been their agreement on so many things. That and her face. It was full of sensuality and energy, very impressive. She had been a rebel. God had been one of the early casualties. They had spent many of their first meetings sharing their hatred of Irish Catholicism. They had a huge long litany which was almost inexhaustable: scapulars, rosaries, confessions, communions, indulgences, prohibitions, aspirations, sins, masses, bowings, bells, candles, scrapings, *mea culpas*, *mea maxima culpas*, mortal sins, hell, priests, nuns, holy hours, processions, shamrocks, holy wells, churchings, god boxes, three Hail Marys for Holy purity, the rhythm method, etcetera. Where religion had come from had engaged endless hours of speculation. He always quoted the chapter and verse of atheism: it was fear that first made gods in the world, and the religion that followed was nothing but submission to mystery. It was the sum of scruples that impeded the free exercise of our faculties. She always gave as an example the belief in the west of Ireland about acne. If you had acne watch for a falling star. As the star fell wipe your face. All eruptions would vanish. If they didn't it was because you were not quick enough.

Julia's voice came from another world. 'Flanagan is cutting a stone, it will be black pearl granite. It's dear but it's the least we can do for the girl. I didn't like the limestone. Flanagan has a machine in from America that can cut a picture of the crucifixion on the granite, all on its own, for an extra hundred pounds. It would have taken an old stonemason a month to do it and he wouldn't do it half as good.' He stopped chewing and looked at her. Her eyes were polished from recent crying. Any minute she could start again. She was brave and it had been her only daughter. He leaned towards her and said gently but firmly: 'No crucifixions, no crosses, just her name: Emer de Brún, 1953-1985 and the words:

> Sunset and evening star,
> And one clear call for me!
> And may there be no moaning of the bar,
> When I put out to sea.'

She looked down at the ground and fought off the tears. 'What in the honour of God does that mean? What bar? Whose bar?'

He told her they were favourite lines of Emer's from Tennyson.

'And who around here is going to know that for God's sake?'

'I will and that's enough,' he said.

She got up from the table and busied herself about the sink. Idleness she knew brought the wrong kind of emotion. He felt that there was quite a lot of unnecessary splashing. She stopped and looked out into the garden above the counter.

'It was a shameful thing that both of you never darkened the door of a church.'

'What would we go in for?'

'To pray for your immortal souls of course.'

'We might as well play hornpipes to a couple of signposts.'

'It was a mistake not to. She knows it now.'

'How dare you say that about her. How dare you,' he shouted in anger. Terrifying images from his childhood suddenly erupted in his mind. The face of a cruel God with a curling lip saying to the soul of a sinner a few seconds after death: 'Depart from me you cursed, into the everlasting flames of hell.' He could protect her while on earth but he was helpless against a divine maniac, a hell packer.

'You shouldn't talk like that about her, she never harmed the hair of anyone's head.'

But the woman was not to be intimidated.

'I'll say what I like about her. It was I who brought her into the light of day, nursed her, loved her, spoiled her. She is as much mine as yours. But she belongs to neither now. She is God's. What'll she say to Him when He asks her why she never even baptised that poor child up in the bed?'

She splashed more water around defiantly. He just stopped himself in time from telling her to leave. But what was the point of a religious argument. It was the same all over Ireland. Men without hope for the good things of this world clung to the promise of the next. Superstition was part of their quotidian. And each day as Ireland grew poorer the beasts of Lough Derg slithered eastward more and more. It was his duty as a member of the minute educated classes to raise the standards of reason and to clash with the forces of evil. But Julia saw some advantage in his failure to reply and she pressed it.

'And no first communion. The day that every child in the parish is leppin' with joy you took the child to the Zoo in Dublin. She'll answer to the Lord for that I'll tell you. Monkeys insteaad of the grace of God.'

He leaped up from the table.

'Enough is enough. That's it. I'm going to ask you to leave this house now Julia – this minute.'

She looked suddenly crushed and she sat down at the table.

'Yes, yes,' she gulped as she fought back the tears, 'I want to leave too. But I can't.' She looked about the kitchen. 'It's this place, her cups, her saucers, it's all I've got that reminds me of her. And all her clothes in the wardrobe.' She pulled a handkerchief out of her sleeve and dabbed her eyes. 'My advice to you is to get rid of all her clothes – anything that reminds you of her that you don't need. Give them to the poor.'

'Certainly not,' he said. 'I like being reminded of her.'

'You should heed what the old people say about these things. Get rid of her clothes, shoes, perfume, otherwise they'll drive you mad. The old people have wisdom as old as the fields.'

He began to understand Julia better each time she opened her mouth. She wasn't a person anymore, just a mobile parish-lore unit that consulted the *is* of the moment with the *should* of local tradition and matched them up willy-nilly.

'Everything stays as it is.'

'Have it your own way then.'

'I will.' He would just, especially the light blue frock with the Helen-of-Troy sleeves that revealed chinks of skin made golden in the Mediterranean sun. Suddenly she was splashing again; that meant she was about to have another go at him.

'You're going to have to think about what you're going to do. I mean you and the child.'

He detested the peasant way of referring to a young boy as a boy but a young girl as a child, even though she was seven. It offended.

'We'll manage quite well thank you,' he said.

'Well, I'm sorry but you're not managing too well at the moment. The child is out of her mind with loneliness.'

'We'll both have to get over it.'

'It's not going to be easy for her. She needs a woman.'

He glanced across at her sharply. 'Meaning?' he said testily.

She grabbed a tea towel and wrapped it round her wet fingers. 'Would you not think of letting the child back to Ballinamawnach with me for a few months. She will get the care and loving attention of six women. It would be good for her. Women need women in times like this. A man is no good.' There was pleading in her voice.

He looked at her for a long time just to make sure she was serious. Such an act would be to condemn the girl to the world of the pishogue, magic, the attitudes of the culturally deprived, hobgoblins, a world of enslavement for women, a world of slyness and rascally brutality for men. 'No!' He said firmly. 'We will adjust in good time. Róisín has the resources of her mother. She is intelligent and adaptable.'

'She is only seven years old. She wouldn't even know the meaning of these words. Give her at least a month in Ballinamawnach.'

Yes, and she'd come back with miraculous medals sewn into her clothes. It would be like 'taking the soup' in reverse. He arose from the table and thanked her for the meal. He said he was going up to tell Róisín her usual story. Julia reminded him that she was in his bed, refusing to go into her own. Then she turned back to the dishes.

It was a four-poster that had gone for a bargain at the auction of furniture of the last of the Bingham-Woods at Killscorna House. He peeped at her from the doorway, clutching her teddy fiercely, white-faced and so alone in the big expanse of bed. Her eyes were large and puzzled. It occurred to him that he had hardly seen her in the past few days – since the Trouble – she was still in shock. He pushed open the door and beamed at her as he moved up to the bed. 'Hi, honey,' he said, 'come into my heart and pick sugar. Any kiss for Dally?' He leaned over and pecked her on the cheek.

'Hallo, Dally,' she said without a trace of warmth. She clutched her teddy all the more and he thought he noticed an imperceptible move away from him into the pillows. He searched his mind for the small talk that is the essential currency of getting through to children. He was always uneasy when alone in her presence, never having mastered the subtlety of the child's imagination.

'You look lovely in your pyjamas, you know that, just lovely. Do you remember where you got them first?' Suddenly he realized his mistake. Emer had pounced on the psychedelic floral pattern in Sacramento last summer. It had been a sunny carnival of McDonalds, Disneyland, the ice-cream parlours. Now, damn, he had done it as he watched her eyes cloud over and then precipitate into a mist of tears.

'Where is Mommy. I want Mommy, what have they done with her. They said she's sick. I'm afraid Dally – I want her.'

He almost reeled. He looked open-mouthed at the hurt innocence of her eyes. Jesus Christ in heaven, had nobody told the child her mother was dead. Now what am I going to do. He walked to the window to think as fast as he could but all he could think of was how swift the night approached from Cloon Wood. It was late autumn. The house shivered. He walked back to the bed and looked down at the quietly weeping child. She was the sole issue of atheists. And atheism was merely to bite the bitter truth. Out, out, hobgoblins! He cleared his throat. 'Róisín, pet, Mommy is no longer with us.'

The child tried to focus on his face, tried to wring meaning out of his words but failed. 'What do you mean? What do you mean?' she whispered aghast. 'I want Mommy to tuck me in.' She almost wailed the last words.

He gulped and looked around the room. He knew it was brutal. But children had to have teeth pulled, the quicker the better.

'You remember Shaska, the dog?'

There was the faintest flicker of recognition. 'Yes, Shaska was a nice dog.'

'That's right, he was a nice dog, but he died, and we buried him in the garden, in the ground. Shaska is no longer with us.' He waited for that to sink in. He was sure it wasn't too obtuse. The child hugged her teddy all the more fiercely and backed farther into the large pillows, away from him.

'Is Mommy under the ground?' She looked at him as if he were a ghost. She was a bright child, he thought, she got the message, thank God for that.

'Yes,' he said simply.

'Will I ever see her again?'

He paused as he mastered all his strength. 'No,' then quietly, 'never again.'

She looked up slowly at him, her tears gone, with an open uncomprehending expression on her face. It was at this precise moment that he saw for the first time the resemblance between her and her mother. Emer had sort of looked like that at times, such as when he tried to explain to her how he made bridges that wouldn't fall down.

'Why never again? What did I do?' She cried again quietly: 'What did I do wrong? Why won't you let me see her Dally, please Dally, just once?'

He needed his wife badly now, even more than the child. What would he say. Words were summoned to his lips, each more useless than the next. Words from a brave world. Words from the world of storm-trooping humanity. But the world of a six-year-old was equally valid.

'Róisín, little apple, Dally is going to look after you. We are alone but we are together – we're going to be happy.'

'Mommy,' the child said dumbly. 'Just Mommy, I don't want you Dally.'

'It's going to be alright, Cherry. I'm going to look after you.' He picked her out of the pillows and put his arms around her, hugging her tightly. She began to wail for her mother all the more, her body bundled into tautness. Then the wail turned to sobs which made her body convulse in his embrace. He became frightened. He had never seen her like this before. The sobs became gasps. He thought she was having a fit. He ran for the door, opened it, and shouted: 'Julia!' But she was there outside the door, waiting. She took her from him. He noticed how the child relaxed and clung to her granny.

'I told you she needed women. Now go and take a walk and leave her to me.'

He moved downstairs and out into the garden. He was shaken by this first enounter with his daughter. It made him feel helpless. He wondered if he was about to become a wreck. Without Emer would he revert to irresponsible bachelor drinking with the boys and going to discos. He shuddered. His memory of those days was a mindless *carpe diem* of pints of stout and sexual exploits. He looked about the garden. It was almost dark, but he could make out her half-built rockery, her fountain, her vegetable patch, all hers; he began to realize that his life had been mostly hers and that without her it would automatically collapse. He was in dread of not being able to cope. He was trapped in this garden, trapped in the half-realized plans of someone now gone. Torment took control and steered him across the road and up on Shanahan's field. He could no longer see the cattle but he was close enough to them to hear their heavy breath shake the dew off the grass. He hoped that distance from the house would give him peace. He decided that if he could walk to the end of Shanahan's field without thinking of her once it would be the beginning of independence. After ten successful steps he felt it reminded him of the ruined church of St Fachtna, where it was commonly believed that if you could walk around it three times without once thinking of a woman you would be assured of eternal salvation. Everybody tried it but most gave up honestly after a few steps. The few who achieved it were accused of being homosexual, for which they would be damned all the more. Emer had dismissed it as a typical expression of ecclesiastical chauvinism. Damn, that did it, he had thought of her. He stopped in the middle of the field and turned round. In the distance a light shone from the upstairs window. Somebody drew the curtain, nearby a cow belched. He was afraid. Now he knew he was afraid they'd get the child. He was afraid he wouldn't be man enough on his own. He decided then to march back and take control of his own house, to establish his own word as the only law. However, before he would march back he would march forward a little more because he needed time to think. Soon he found himself at the edge of Cloon wood. He ventured in till his eyes grew accustomed to the total dark. He leaned his back against a tree and peered at the distant window through the twigs. He moved deeper in and then he turned to look again. Nothing. It was a beginning.

Later he wandered into the kitchen and sat beside the big range. Julia was knitting beside the table. No word passed between them. After a while she coughed and said, 'Wouldn't you think of taking off your shoes – they're sodden – leave them there near the range – they'll be dry in the morning.'

She couldn't keep it in, he thought. Years of fighting damp, of outmanoeuvering draughts, of sitting in the shade in summer – all punctuated with cups of tea – had dulled her mind to all other sensibilities.

'They're sodden and I'm glad of it,' he said, and he spread his feet in front of him in order to observe the water trickle onto the floor.

'That's all very fine now. But you might have a cold tomorrow, where would you be then? A chill is the beginning of the end of us all. That's what happened Jack, God rest him.'

He thought of her husband, a silent man who had spent his time on this earth walking about the haggard with bucketfuls of this, that and the other.

'I thought he died of cancer.' There was the smallest trace of malice in his words. She almost dropped the knitting.

'None of our family ever died of cancer. He got cancer alright but it was pneumonia that got him in the end.' She said it with a certain note of triumph. You had to be careful how you lived in Ireland but you had to be even more careful that you didn't die of the wrong disease. She continued to knit. Click, clack, went the needles, never dropping a stitch. He listened to the sparring needles in a bemused fashion until it occurred to him that something was wrong. Suddenly he knew what it was. The clock, the big two-hundred year old

Dublin regulator was stopped. It had been an extravagant purchase of Emer's in the early days. She had always kept it wound up.

'The clock is stopped,' he said. She didn't look up at him but continued to knit. He got up and walked to the corner where it stood, mute as a milestone. As he reached for the key, she said, 'Would you not think it would be a great honour to the dead to let the clock hold its peace for a month?' He thought about it. Killing the clock, gramophone, and radio for a month was a commonplace practice. But it was superstition and had he and Emer not fought superstition as ruthlessly as Julia had fought damp and chills. Anyway, it had a grand generous tick and tock which had punctuated the happiest years of his life. He wound it up slowly. Then he had to move the hands and realised his mistake as the clock chimed all the way up to 10.00 p.m. It chimed all over the house, in each chime a message he daren't interpret. Then it settled down to its tick, tock. He sat beside the range again fearing he could do nothing right. His feet were freezing but he couldn't take his shoes off now, it would be a defeat, in spite of the fact that everything she said made sense. He glanced at her out of the corner of his eye. Did he imagine she had a self-satisfied look about her. He was sure of it. She'd have to go that was all – he'd manage quite well without her. He would master basic cooking in a few days – laundry and things like that would not be too difficult he decided. Beyond that there was little else to housework. Still, he'd have to go back to work the following day because the bridge over the new by-pass was reaching a critical stage and the subcontractors were beginning to give hassle. Maybe he'd let her stay a few days, maybe even a week. His feet were so cold he had to get up and stamp the floor. He walked to the clevy and took down a bottle of Crested Ten.

'Would you like a drink?' he said as a truce gesture.

'A solitary drop of that stuff has never dampened a tooth in my head and never will till the day I go under.'

'O.K.,' he said as he poured himself a very large whiskey. He tossed it all back neat in rare abandon, winced and then waited for it to expand within. It did, and he exhaled in gratitude.

'I've heard it said many a time that a man in the grip of fresh sorrow would be better off to go dry at least until he is on his old mettle again,' she said blinking between stitches. You're as dry as an old limeburner's boot yourself he said to himself as he topped up his glass again.

'All my life I've watched men drink their way through farms and fields.'

'For Christ's sake, Julia, give me a break. You're playing the tune the old black cow died of.'

'That's all very well to say that today,' she said, 'but where will it all end. That's what I'd like to know. Where will it all end?'

Emer, girl, he said to himself, you were a sparkling trout out of the genetic cesspool – the others were all perch and pike. All your brothers and your mother are fatheads. They all live and you die – another proof that God does not exist.

'Look what happened to Paky Connor,' she said.

'Who's Paky Connor?' he asked in desperation.

'He was a second, no a third cousin of my own dear Jack, God rest him. He was going out with a no-good hussy of a girl who left him down. It was the luck of God that she did for if she had married him there would be no end to the calamity. She was a stupid ignorant gligeen who wouldn't know B from a bull's foot or C from a chest of drawers. Anyway, he took to the drink until he got himself and the farm into such a state that one night they had to tie him to a chair until the van called for him.'

'What van, for God's sake?'

She put her knitting down on her lap and looked at him as if he were a tramp who called to the back door. 'The van from the mental asylum of course. He's in there to this day and I'll tell you one thing for sure, he's living a very dry life.' She resumed her knitting. 'The brothers signed him in and I'll tell you thing for sure, if they ever sign him out, 'tis out in a box he'll come.'

He looked at her openmouthed. 'And I suppose the brothers are looking after the farm.'

'Yes,' she said, 'It's as green as holly and not a buachalán or a weed in sight.'

He poured himself another whiskey. 'That man was just suffering from a nervous breakdown, it's disgraceful that he should spend all his life in the asylum.'

'Well, that's one name for it, but we call it going insane. Thanks be to God for mental asylums or the countryside wouldn't be safe for a body.'

'Jesus, sweet Jesus,' was all he said. What a paradox was Ireland he mused. His job called for a mastery of the most up-to-date computer technology, but at night he'd have to come home to this bronze age view of life. What a pity machines couldn't change people. He knew that in the year 2087 things would be just the same. Tools and machines might change but they would never lick the bronze age. He got up and corked the bottle and put it back in the clevy.

'Well I'm going to bed,' he said. 'I'll have peep in at Róisín and see how she's doing. I might tell her that story if she's awake.'

Julia became as alert as a cat, dropped her knitting and said in a threatening tone: 'Wouldn't you be advised by one in the know and leave well alone.'

'How do you mean?'

'She's satisfied now, she's in her own bed. If you go in now you'll start the whole thing again.' He resented her tone and the implication of her control. If he left her away with this she'd have him wandering around the place with buckets, same as she had her unfortunate husband.

'I'll see you, good night,' he said and trudged up the stairs.

The night light burned beside her bed and she lay between the sheets clutching her teddy and sucking her thumb. Her eyes darted towards him but no flicker of joy appeared as it used before. He moved quietly up to her bed and bent down over her. Her eyes were focussed somewhere in the dark part of the room.

'How about a little kiss for Dally?' he said as he nudged her teddy.

She continued to suck for a minute without looking at him. All of a sudden she raised herself up on her elbow and said accusingly to him: 'Daddy, you told me a lie.'

'Why don't you call me Dally, as you used to?'

'Cause, Gran said that was wrong, only babies say Dally, it's Daddy.'

He felt like rushing downstairs and throwing Julia out into the garden for good.

'Call me Dally. Now what lie did I tell you?'

'You said Mommy was like Shaska in the ground.'

He sat down beside her gently hardly daring to ask her what she meant. 'I'm afraid she is pet. That's the way it is and we must put up with it.'

She backed away from him, a hurt look crossing her face. 'She is not, she is not. She is in heaven with Holy God and all the holy angels.' She presented him with the left side of her jaw in defiance. The thumb popped in for three more sucks then out again. 'And if anybody goes near me or hits me she'll send an angel down to stop him.' The thumb was jammed back for refuel.

He never knew how to react quickly when taken by surprise – it was a failing. He began to stammer, then stopped himself and asked coldly: 'Who told you this nonsense?'

'Gran,' she said defiantly but her mouth quivered with lack of conviction. Then she continued but there was pleading in her tone as tears began to spring at the corners of her eyes. 'She is up there now and she is looking down at the two of us and she is laughing – and one day Gran and me and you will die and we'll go up to her – and we'll have a great time. Isn't that true Daddy, please Daddy?' Her little face quivered shades of hope, loss, and shaky defiance. Her thumb went in and she looked up expectantly at him. He looked at her but he hadn't the courage to hold her eye. He took her hand in his, it was as limp as a sock. 'The fact is,' he said, 'the fact is,' but he didn't know what the fact was, except that he was tired and would have to put an end to this once and for all. 'The fact is, I'll have to close the window because you'll get cold.' He got up and crossed the room and looked out onto the garden. There was nothing to be seen except a moth which banged against the windowpane to escape the autumn chill. 'The window is shut already,' the child said. 'And so it is,' he said and came back slowly and sat down with a sigh beside her.

'Look, we've got to be brave about this you and me,' he took her hand again but she pre-empted any strategy by starting to cry out loud. He had no defence against tears. Once only Emer had to resort to them and he conceded the universe. As for a crying child he usually handed it over to a woman. But he wasn't going for Julia again. He took her in his arms and this time she did not resist. But she continued to cry and sob. 'Sure Mommy isn't out in the cold ground?' she pleaded.

He hadn't considered that aspect of it, it could be upsetting for a child. Anyway Mommy was nowhere.

'Mommy is not out in the cold ground.'

'And she is not where Shaska is.'

'No.'

He could feel her relaxing in his arms. She was soft, cuddly and yielding. She put her thumb in her mouth and sucked on this new confirmation. After a while she asked only just a little tearfully: 'She is in heaven with Holy God?'

Heaven was a mere metaphor for the dark eternity of non-existence. Children above all needed metaphors. Santa Claus was one, so were witches. He had never questioned stories about witches and magic before, why heaven now. A witch was a metaphor for the forces of hazard. We were all victims of hazard.

'Yes,' he said almost inaudibly, 'she is in heaven.' He was an atheist who felt he had just committed mortal sin.

'Why didn't you tell me that before? Gran was right.'

'Call me Dally,' he said simply.

'And is heaven full of angels?'

'Yes.'

'And will they look after me if I cut my knee?'

'Yes.'

'And is Mommy laughing?'

'Yes.' He felt like a thieving dog. What had he stolen? He had stolen away truth and put in its place a lie, hoping that it would not be discovered. It was the same as stealing his wife away from life and putting in her place some rags and bones. He felt he was stuffing the effigy of Emer de Brún in the name of peace. The crying had stopped now. She sucked peacefully beside him.

'What dress is she wearing?'

'What do you mean?'

'In heaven. Now.'

'She's wearing a new dress. It's pink and long and sways as she walks.' He had bought it for her fifty billion years ago way out in the Crab Nebula and she would wear it for all eternity and it would always blow gently about her legs in the cosmic breeze. The child was asleep. And religion was born. Only five days gone and already philosophy had caved in at the knees. They had vanquished. Heaven had arrived. Hell would follow in its own good time. They had vanquished because he was not strong. It was this more than anything else made him cry, slowly at first just the way a mist becomes rain. Then he cried freely and all the coldness of the last few days turned hot and flowed with ease down his cheek. It was good to cry. It was warm. It was warm also to think of her in heaven and not in the cold cold ground. She had a favourite proverb for calamity. 'If the skies were to fall we'd catch larks.' Well the skies had fallen, and he had caught a lark – a lark from the clear air: now he knew where religion came from. From children. All the great philosophers had been wrong. Spëgler, Schleiermacher, Remach, Murray, Ellis. It was to appease the child. At least he had borne that much from the fray.

He held her in his arms and looked out the window. There was but one star shining. It shone like a cat's eye from under a bed. It was an evening for oneness, one star, one man, one child, one lost love, one lark from the clear air. And one faith. Faith in the goodness of man and no more. He felt himself repeat her favourite lines.

> Twilight and evening bell
> And after that the dark
> And may there be no sadness of farewell
> When I embark.

Nell

I knew the crows were there; their shadows circled the plough before they dropped out of the sky, slow and silent as black snow. They had not come to feed on the fresh earth, for their craws were gorged with the day's thieving. They had come to gloat. Their black eyes glinted in the evening sun as they watched my team of horses and swishing plough slice the green onto the brown. I stumbled along the furrow in fear, for their presence always announced the coming of The Bat O'Shea, my master. My boyish hands gripped both reins and handles and I felt the power of the plough go shuddering through my bones. I prayed I wouldn't hit a rock.

When I came to the headland I saw the dog for the first time. She was standing on a rock in the rough land above the ditch, her nose winding the faint mysteries of the valley. She was a tri-colour shepherd, black back, brown apron and leggings, white face. I knew she was a stranger, for strangers have a way of knowing each other and I knew she saw me too. Suddenly, as if startled, she leapt gracefully away into the hollies.

'That's a nice way to earn your bread, staring up at the mountains; 'tis the likes of you has the likes of me plundered.' His nagging tone deflated me. That I should stare at anything other than horse, furrow, and plough was a fault The Bat would cure me of. He stood on the ditch, perpendicular and forbidding, a holly stick under his arm; and his black coat thrown over his shoulder made him look as if he had swooped down from the dark clouds.

'That first furrow's as bent as a butcher's hook and the others are hooking with it. People are going to say The Bat can't plough, you fool.' He spat on the ground. 'Better hit no rock.' He bounded off the ditch and was gone.

I spat on the ground also for I was at an impressionable age; then I coaxed the horses into the next furrow. I glanced up at the hollies and the withered fern. Nothing moved. I needed companionship badly, but people would not do anymore. I picked up stones and flung them at the crows, but, like flies upon a dunghill, they acknowledged me with only token displacement.

I looked down at the Black Valley that had been appointed by law and nature to be my prison. A year previously I had been orphaned and my relatives had taken me from the town. They dumped me in the valley saying, 'Look at the beauty of the country, lad. Why, you'll become healthy and, who knows, you might learn to plough and things like that.' The last I saw of them was a pony-trap full of red faces and sly nudges escaping down the road and I knew they would remain for evermore what the lawyer said they were: distant relatives. They also took my dog.

Beauty they said; the only beauty I saw was the river curling like an old horsewhip on the valley floor before it escaped for ever this shadowy corner of the earth; for indeed the valley was a conspiracy of watery shadows that always outmanoeuvred the sun. I was the victim of blackness – shadow, crow and valley.

That night when I got back from the fields I watched their dark faces bulging with boiled eggs and bastible bread, and thought better of mentioning the dog. When they arose from the table I sat down and finished what they had left. A candle was lit and a jug and loaf danced on the whitewashed wall. The clock's slow rhythm told of a house of silence.

They had given me the room farthest from the fire; for this I was grateful for I was never disturbed. I shot the bolt, lit my candle and let my eyes shine on the familiar objects that I looked on as my own. It was as private as a wood. In the corner lay a huge heap of wheat, dull gold in the poor light. Sometimes after the day's toil and insults I would throw myself upon it, burying my face and limbs in it, letting the weariness of my bones trickle down through the cool grain. By my bed was a book chest, its old wood and books smelling of places I would never see.

I stood by the window and searched the sky for my secret stars; stars so little they wouldn't be missed out of the sky, nor would they be owned in error by others like me. They were still there. A secret is a lovely thing.

Across the valley I could see the lights of the cabins. I wondered emptily about them. I knew what they would look like inside: a man, a dog, a clock, and severe religious faces that danced out from the walls to the flickering candle.

My bed was a brass one, wherever they got it. I don't know why they let me have it, maybe they felt guilty about my clothes, my small helpings. I threw myself on it and slept, secure in the knowledge that for the time being stone walls, oaken door, and double thatch would keep me safe.

Next day I saw her in the sallies, her fur flaming in the shadows. I didn't approach her because I knew she was making up her mind. I wasn't surprised when on the following morning she was at the front gate. We all approached within twenty feet of her; I was jealous of the others' interest in her, but I could hardly shout 'I saw her first'. The cowhouse door banged and The Bat thumped across the cobbles, every second step muffled on fresh cowdung. His clothes were covered with a confetti of hayseed and straw.

'Somebody's lost his dog and not from this parish,' he barked, the strain of words visible on his face. He wiped the sweat from his brow with his filthy cap. 'He might stay with us, we need a dog,' he said to his wife. He didn't call her Gubby, she didn't call him Bat.

'He'll stay with us if he's any use,' she said with finality, her words making no impression on the mouth that years of sourness had weighed down at the corners.

'I'll get him,' said Timmy, the son, and darted forward. The dog wheeled and flashed down the boreen about thirty yards before stopping again. She didn't show fear and I knew she was teaching these yokels a sense of reserve.

'You'll frighten him,' said Gubby, and she began to shout hoarsely: 'Here pup, here pup, that's a nice pup.' Her falsetto flushed blackbirds out of all the ditches and the dog stiffened.

'Go in and bring out the rabbit bones,' The Bat said. The rule was that when nobody was named the 'boy' should do it. I turned towards the house, leaving the three of them whistling and bawling at the dog; three calves on the dunghill silently watched. I knew better than to tell them that rabbit bones could kill a dog as quick as broken bottles. It was no wonder they couldn't keep a dog. In the kitchen I got rid of the deadly splintered bones and stuffed my pockets with bacon fat and bread.

The Bat grabbed the plate and threw a bone to the dog. She had vanished round the bend before it hit the ground. 'You were too late with them bones, you layabout.' I didn't spit on his face for my mouth was dry; I could have struck him with the pike, but a small heart has a small courage. I marched down the boreen without their permission; I knew she would be waiting for me round the bend. I broke a knob of bacon fat in front of her and watched her eyes melt with desire; her drooling muzzle eased it out of my hand and then she wolfed it back. She licked my palm and fingers until they were hot and sticky. While she ate the bread from the ground I felt her condition. She was only fur and bones and had been at least a fortnight on the mountains. There was no need to coax her back and I knew she was following me for I heard her nails scrape on stone like holly leaves in a breeze.

The three were still there, eyeing us suspiciously, blocking our entrance. 'How'd you catch him?' 'What were you doing round the bend?' 'Will he bite?' they muttered together, unsure of the new situation. 'She's a bitch, and her name is Nell,' I said calmly and I marched past them. I didn't know why I called her Nell for I never knew anyone of that name.

I was given a scythe and banished to the bog to cut rushes. As I left the haggard I heard the rabbit bones snap like barley sugar. All day I spent mowing rushes, each sweep of the keen blade destroying the green things at my feet. Destruction sweetens a bitter heart. No whistle was blown for me to come to dinner; instead Gubby hobbled over a ditch with cold tea in a can and dry bread. I sat on the rushes munching the bread and sipping from the can. Gubby had the eyes of a dead mackerel as she surveyed the rushes and the bread, the rushes and the tea, her lips bloodless from a lifetime's strain of such small comparisons.

If she would only speak to me first I would ask her about my dog. In vain I waited for a word to crack the drooping mouth line. And I said nothing for I was old enough to know that people would use my feelings as they did my muscle and bone. For the rest of the day Nell was heavy on my mind. Would she forget me, would others get to her first?

When I got back to the haggard a ball of fur catapulted itself at me from under the lilacs, dancing all round me, licking my hands and face. I patted her big white head and the loyal memory within it. I straightened up and walked proudly up the haggard; for the first time in that cursed place I had support.

The Bat and Timmy were standing in the hayshed, the breeze wrapping stray straws around their feet. 'If frolicking is all she can do, she'll go out that gate quicker than she came in.' His tone was always rough but in the presence of his son it was threatening. Nell was cowed by his words and hung at my heels. 'I'll bring in the cows,' I said, and headed for the bog. I could only imagine what had happened between Nell and The Bat, for it was a valley of idiots who could command neither man, dog, nor beast. Often I watched them, red-faced, waving their sticks, cursing into the wind, their wild shouts confounding both dog and beast. Bawlers the lot of them. The way men handled their dogs was my way of knowing fools. That evening I watched her scent the bounds of the farm, the cows, the gates, her nose flooding her memory with things to be remembered.

That night I took down a brush and cloth and began to work on her, rubbing hard along her back, coaxing the faintest gloss from her thick coat. I teased out the matted feathers, then the scruff. The Bat was watching me darkly from the hearth. 'What in God's name are you doing with that dog, boy?' I slackened my efforts as I sought the right answer, for his tone told me I had somehow broken the rules. 'A well-groomed dog takes pride in herself and works better that way.'

'Dogs don't give a damn how they look, you stump of a fool. Anyway, what would the likes of you know about dogs.'

'My father told me,' I lied, knowing that even in this wretched valley the memory of the dead was sacred. He grunted and got up and strolled down to the doorway, resting his elbows on the half-door. He did this often and somehow it made me feel safe. Maybe his staring for hours into the dark gulf of the valley calmed him and refined a patient ease out of his brutal nature; maybe the darkness of his soul took comfort and fellowship from the night that thickened beyond the threshold. Or perhaps the lighted windows from across the glen teased his memory for how things were and gave him inklings of how they might have been.

That night when Timmy had crawled up to the half-loft, and the old couple departed with their candle to the room, dragging their weary shadows after them, I raided the kitchen. My knife hacked at pigs' cheeks, hams from the rafters, knuckle bones from the pickle barrel, anything that wouldn't be missed.

The softness of the bedclothes excited Nell's playful instincts; she romped and wallowed on them, waving her legs in the air, matching her rich coat to the patchwork quilt and all the time yelping impishly. I fed her, making sure to keep some of the choicest bits till last. 'What we've got is class, Nell, class.' She nodded in assent and went on eating. 'We're going to show these yokels a thing or two.' She considered this and licked my fingers noisily in agreement. And so, with such sounds, I drifted off to sleep, the little sounds of intrigue, friendship, progress.

That week Nell and I showed them; anything that was herdible we did it together – goats, calves, stray donkeys, cows, dry cattle, tinkers' ponies. They allowed me to become more my own boss because they were pleased. The dog was mine although they owned both of us. I was jealous of her glances, but I needn't have been because she would only come to my whistle, had only eyes for me, and followed me everywhere. I was somebody; I had four swift feet to do my bidding, a deep bark to announce my will, and sharp teeth to compensate for my size. I was proud; I was showing them.

The Bat had sheep on the mountain, but they hadn't been dipped or shorn in three years because they could not be caught. They were the blackfaced mountainy kind, wild and light as paper-bags in a storm. We brought them down. Towards evening, tired but triumphant, we drove them into the haggard, all forty of them. They were crazed by the civilisation of man, dog and buildings. Wild-eyed, they exploded into the air at the slightest sound. The Bat, Gubby and Timmy came flying out of the house, almost trampling each other with excitement. Straight away they began to count them, their high-pitched yelps mixing with the frightened bleats. 'One, two, three, four, five, six, seven, Christ, mind that ram, fourteen, fifteen, sixteen, I've counted them ones already, twenty, twenty-one, twenty-two, shut up I can't hear myself, eight, nine, ten, eleven. Jaysus deliver me I'll have to shtart again.' 'They're all there,' I shouted with command. There was silence in the haggard.

They noticed us for the first time. The Bat came forward awkwardly and bent down over the dog. 'Well, well, Nelly girl, we might keep you for another little while, after all.' I didn't mind that he should choose to ignore me, but that he should call my dog Nelly made me rage within.

That night Nell and I talked ourselves to sleep. 'We have 'em now, Nell, we have 'em on the run. Yes, we'll take no more old guff from the crowd above.' She snuggled up close to me. 'Yes, me and you make a great team. We'll leave the valley and go down to the sea. There's great money to be made out of fish down by the sea.'

When she came into heat I watched her night and day, for there was no dog in the parish good enough for her. Timmy had been watching me for some time. I didn't encourage him, however, becauses I knew what was on his mind: he wanted a share in the dog. He stopped me up at the hollies one day.

'Would you teach me to whistle, please?'

'Why?'

'Ah, I'd like to be heard far away.'

'It's very hard, it takes years to learn.'

'I don't care how long, I want to be able to whistle like you.'

'It's going to be very hard, you're missing a tooth.'

Timmy was a year older than me, but he was soft and honest. I didn't dislike him. Now he fingered the gap with such disappointment that I relented. 'Well, you'll be able to whistle alright, but it will always be a bit hollow.' I gave him a half-hearted lesson and left him at it.

The December fair came round. Long before dawn Nell and I went to the bog to fetch the cattle. Frost had scoured the skies of cloud and sealed the pools with silvery lids which the heavy beasts crunched loudly, their steaming breath dusting the way in front of them. Back at the yard The Bat and Timmy were dressed in collars and ties. I felt ashamed of my blue knees which peeped out over my wellington tops. Gubby came out with a list of messages, warnings, and threats. 'Don't ye dare come home with them, sell well, do you hear me? Get yeerselves boots.'

I stamped my cold feet, whistled up Nell and moved onto the road. Holly, furze, and mountain ash gradually gave way to elm, oak, sycamore as we dropped down on the good land. Through the bare branches we saw the cracked saucer of moon heading east across the mountains. Passing the rookery of Cloon I could barely see the outline of the crows roosting in the trees. They looked as if somebody had spent the night decorating the tree-tops with old boots. I laughed and dragged my feet through the frozen leaves. They crackled like eggshells.

The streets gladdened my heart, they were so thronged with people, carts and cattle. The smell of frying rashers, and whiskey, the barking of dogs, and the handshakes of laughing farmers made me feel good.

We stationed the cattle outside a pub, their nostrils steaming up the window through which their lonesome eyes watched the red faces lining the counter. Timmy, Nell and I hemmed them in. I bought a currany bun and gave most of it to Nell.

All morning a procession of buyers moved up and down the fair, their jabbing sticks not only testing the condition of the cattle, but probing deeply for flaws in the sellers, the inexperienced, the timid, the desperate. Twice The Bat wavered, twice he held; differences were almost split only to hold at a stubborn half-crown; his sourness always won the day. Timmy and I were frozen, longed for the warmth of a shop, longed for a bite of food, longed for a bargain struck.

After midday light rain killed the cold but soaked me to the skin. Mist swirled down the street, quieting the bustle and dulling the outline of things. Coloured shop lights glowed through it, reflecting on the watery beads that gathered on the backs of the cattle. I bought three biscuits with red icing on them and gave them to Nell. It gave me pleasure to see a thing of mine enjoy itself so much.

The Bat went into the pub. We waited. Timmy stood above the cattle, steam rising from his black overcoat. 'I think he'll sell now,' I shouted across to him. He smiled back. I hoped that drink would make The Bat drop his guard with the next buyer.

The day wore on. Cattle seemed to be thinning, or was it the shadows that hid them? The pubs were beginning to fill. Songs, laughter and breaking glass could be heard here and there. Christmas was almost upon us and I was standing in wet cowdung. I suddenly got very cold. I found myself edging to the pub doorway where every so often a draught of warm air blew at my back whenever a customer passed through. Nell moved with me and her rich coat flopped on a dry spot by the window. I thought of food.

Suddenly there was a shout from the road. 'Lucy!' I shot out of my daydream; at the same time Nell streaked from my side with a yelp and jumped on a huge man in a black coat who stood in the middle of the road. I watched in amazement as she danced about him. 'Lucy, you little devil, where did you go to at all?' He took her up in his arms and did a little dance, pleasure shining in his eyes. 'Well, well, sure I thought I'd never see you again.' I stood riveted to the doorway, and I never felt so cold in my life. He was a tall man, powerfully built, a humorous face with bushy eyebrows that jutted out almost as far as the peak of his cap. There was a row of brass army buttons down the front of his coat. He had a whip under his arm. 'Nell,' I said with as much command as I could muster; there was fear and accusation in my voice. She pretended not to hear, the whore. 'Nell,' I screamed with rage at her. This time she slunk over to me, licked my cold hand, fawned for a brief moment and then she was gone.

I leaned against the jamb of the door with weakness. Timmy, sensing the tension in my voice, looked in annoyance at the man. 'Nelly, Nelly,' he said, but the man had by now stooped down to the dog, examining her paws and ears, feeling her condition. Timmy looked urgently at me. 'That's our dog,' he warned the man in the street. The man straightened up and ignoring Timmy strolled over to me. 'Where're ye from?'

'Black Valley.'

'The Valley!' he said, astounded. He pressed his palms to his forehead, eyes shut, lips slowly counting. 'That's twenty miles from Coom any day of the week.' He looked down admiringly at the dog. 'Musha, what brought you down the Valley side?'

I looked at Nell but she wouldn't look at me, the slut. She knew I was looking at her because she pretended to sniff at the roadway at the same time. I also felt Timmy's eyes on me. Cold rage took hold of me and my fist tightened on the holly stick. I could have beaten her all over the fair.

Timmy rushed over and grabbed her by the scruff of the neck. 'She's our dog and she stays with us.' There was outrage in his voice; he looked defiantly at both of us.

The big man smiled down at him. 'Now, now, laddy, don't hurt the poor dog. Look,' he said, 'I'll tell you what I'll do with you. You know that everything knows its own master. Let the dog go, and if she stays with you she's yours and if she comes to me she's mine. There's a bargain for you now.' He spoke evenly, with a smile, and he spoke with charm, which was unusual; strong men don't need it. Timmy looked at me; I was so sick that I couldn't say a word.

The man walked out to the middle of the roadway. Timmy loosed his grip, and immediately she bounded out to him. Timmy was enraged. 'Are you going to let her go with him?' he hissed at me. The question confused me; how could I fight for the thing that had deserted me, even though I loved it.

Timmy didn't wait for an answer. He shot into the pub and emerged shortly with The Bat, wiping froth from his mouth. 'The big tall fellow out there,' he pointed. The Bat's eyes took in the position of the dog and the height of the man. 'Call back your dog, our dog,' he said to me. I was already sick of dogs and men; my courage had long since left me. 'Nell,' I said weakly, but it was more of a statement than an order, because I knew dogs, their loyalties and memories were long and their hearts were simple. She did not acknowledge me.

The Bat leapt out to the middle of the roadway, his jaw almost out of joint with anger. 'Look here, whoever you are, that's our dog there, always was and always will be. Good day to you now.'

The big man's smile never changed even though The Bat said his words insultingly. He looked down at the dog. 'I've reared that dog since she was a puppy; I trained her until she was the best dog in the mountains. One day I lost her and ever since I've been searching hill and valley. Now that I've found her I'm delighted and would like to take her home. I'm greatly beholden to you all.' He spoke so quietly that The Bat was put out; for The Bat's manner was to swamp his fear with bold words and insults.

'Look, I've just told you that she's ours and that's the way it is. You don't think that we'd let every mountainy robber and tramp of the road lay a claim to her.' He stooped down to take the dog, but he was grabbed by the scruff of the neck and almost lifted off his feet. Big sinewy hands shook him so that his arms and legs danced like a puppet, until his filthy cap fell on the street. 'If it weren't that your two sons were here to remember it forever I'd break every bone in your body, you scruff, you.' The man picked up his whip from the roadway, whistled and moved off up the street.

The Bat was shivering all over, short of breath; his eyes were polished with shock and I wondered how somebody so swarthy could pale so quickly. Timmy, shaken, ran out and picked up his father's cap. 'Here, Da, you're not going to let him away with it, Da?' he said anxiously. The Bat was watching the large shoulders disappear into the misty evening.

'Christ, Da, don't mind the bloody dog. Run after him and hit him.' There was a terrible urgency in his voice.

The Bat cleared his throat.

'Go on, Da, hit him quick before he's gone.' Rain washed down over the appealing eyes. The Bat just looked at the road. 'Christ, Da, you're not afraid of him,' the boy wailed.

The blow came so suddenly I only heard it. Timmy was knocked right across to the pub, where he sat on the street with a thud, blood streaming from his nose. 'I'll take no impudence from you, you pup. Mind them cattle like you're supposed to,' and The Bat passed us by into the pub.

I threw my stick on the ground and walked off. I had had enough of farmers, cattle and dogs. I was full of loathing for everything on this earth. I don't know how long I squelched my way through the fair. Every house seemed to be a pub. Through the windows I could see the lines of red-faced farmers at the bar. I envied them their fatness, their satisfaction.

I walked on, accusing, scolding, telling myself what I should have done. At the end of the town they passed me, he on his bike, she trotting behind him. They were going home; no, she was going to his house. I leant on the shaft of a cart and watched them disappear into the dark. What a ridiculous name was Lucy.

As I trudged back the streets were deserted. Only animals with their heads in halters stood around, wasting their lonely eyes on the mist. I felt that I too should be tethered to a street pole. But I couldn't stop thinking of the big man. There was something about him. It wasn't just that he was powerfully built. It was the kindness in his face. For such a man I would work for nothing.

There was a little old man sitting in the rain beside a barrow, his face as wrinkled as the apples he sold. 'Sir, could you tell me where Coom is, please?'

'The place is full of Cooms, which one do you want?'

'Well, this Coom would be in the mountains.'

'They're all in the mountains, tell me more.'

I thought he was doing it for spite. I had no more information to give. 'Well, this man I'm looking for has a big black coat and a bicycle.'

'Yerra, you poor fool, sure they've all got black coats and them that can afford them have bikes,' and he whined with laughter.

I turned away, feeling I had made a fool of myself. I felt his laughter hot on the nape of my neck. I was sure that the whole fair was laughing at me. I hurried through the muck and mist. Oh God! I hated farmers and fairs. Pigs selling cattle to pigs.

When I got back the pair were standing by the cattle. My coming seemed to be a signal for we moved off. Nobody said a word.

We took the winding road to the Valley, wet towels of wind slapping our faces. Over our heads the clouds cleared and I saw the Milky Way wind through the sky. The world was a vast place. Once I had climbed the mountain and had almost cried with joy to see other places on this earth besides the Valley. But when we entered the Valley, that Valley of the Black Pig, the Dark which had not moved awaited us, and I heard the gates of the mountains crash shut behind us, and I knew there would be no escape, for this conspiracy of shadows would always outmanouvre my sun.

A Straight Run Down to Killcash

I saw her for the first time pushing the priests' dinner on a trolley through our lines, her soft white neck drooped over crown of lamb, roast golden potatoes, broccoli clumps, raspberries and cream. She pushed silently through the gamut of adolescent desire, the mouths of the juniors watering, our senior eyes prying the secrecies of her retreating body.

I saw her again in the dormitory with a dustpan, cleaning under our beds. I passed her by and smiled; her eyes, at first uncertain, half-yielded and her lips parted. They were wet. I carried her wet lips on my heart to the studyhall where hundreds of students sat in dry labour. I listened to their pens scratch and pages rustle, and I wrestled with my Odyssey. The long shadow of Fr Shore, the invigilator, sought for Readers Digests, Peter Cheyneys and banned literature among the toiling heads. A memory, to me, is a useless thing; it lacks progression, development. Being a prefect in the A class, I was allowed to whisper for ink and dictionaries. 'O'Connell,' I said, 'who's the new scrubber?' O'Connell, who was fat and indolent, excelled in gossip. He dispatched numerous bits of paper on secret destinations. Later he dropped a grubby note on my desk and my heart quickened to the magic of her name: Sandra. I smiled for I had never met a girl of that name – only in books; little girls called Sandra wore jodhpurs and rode ponies called Black Prince at gymkhanas in rural England. I repeated the name to myself, marvelling at the rightness of its vowels and consonants, at the superiority of two syllables over one; it was a name that had texture and colour; it had wet lips.

We sat at our tables in the refectory in silence. Silence, said Fr O'Shiel, was good because it made for quiet, digestion, and the chance to hear the sacred reading. It was read by Falvey, the head prefect, a sly man from the sly west; he sat huddled on a high rostrum as if he were sheltering from the rain of his bleak mountain parish, and intoned the miracles, wedding feasts and parables with crushing piety. But although he was going for the church, piety didn't blend with his red face and thick speech. And we all watched Sandra; she stood at the bottom of the refectory hall beside piles of pan-loaves, her eyes and hands betraying discomfort in the presence of so many people. As hands shot into the air she delivered loaves to those tables, eyes following her every move.

O'Connell nudged me. 'She's a fine thing. Shorey must have slipped up, she won't last.'

Fr Shore was responsible for recruiting domestic staff. It was said that he travelled the countryside and picked the ugliest. He had climbed over mountains of dung to get Philomena; Theresa he had found in a bog cutting turf. Theresa had huge forearms, purple from washing dishes, which inhibited adolescent forwardness.

'Let's have a bit of fun, Stack,' O'Connell said. 'Ask her for some bread. Get her to stoop down and we'll see what's to see.' There was plenty of bread left. I listened to Falvey's terrible piety and my eyes sought her out. Slowly I raised my hand. She came towards me with the bread and I saw her face start when she recognized me. We did not smile even as our hands barely touched. But something had happened. There was progression. I took the loaf and placed it in front of O'Connell. 'Now eat it,' I said. I noticed Fr O'Shiel's shadow falling on our table. I saw his troubled eyes look in her direction. She did not appear in the refectory again.

I waited for her in the dormitory. It took many days of simulated shavings and shoe-polishings and all the time her name was a perpetual refrain in my mind. She came in with an armful of pillowslips and began to fit them. I walked towards her, one hand in a shoe, the other holding a brush. Her eyes were frightened and she continually glanced at the door. There were keys on the bed; I grabbed them and with the other hand led her quickly out of the dormitory. She kept on asking what I wanted, where I was going, but her hand in mine squeezed secrecies that told of other thoughts. I finally opened the door and bundled her inside. 'Welcome to the Ritz,' I said. We both stopped suddenly and stared. Hundreds of blue-rimmed chamber-pots filled the room, stacked against the day the whole school might come down with flu. I had only heard about it but never imagined it could be like this. We both laughed at those little pots that made the human race look so ridiculous, and as we shared our laughter, I crushed her in a fevered embrace. She kept saying: 'I'll lose my job if the priests catch me.' I took the big heavy key and locked the door. Its metallic click made her feel secure. She relaxed in my arms only to tense again with furious desire. I knew that it would be easy, but as our naked bodies tumbled on the floor and our limbs nudged chamber-pots about, I thanked Christ and heaven for my joy.

The classroom was stuffy as twenty-five seniors and I listened to Fr O'Growney intone his misgivings about the morality of ancient Irish sagas. *Tóraíocht Diarmada agus Gráinne*, which was on the Leaving Certificate course, was a typical example. Gráinne was obviously sleeping with Diarmuid, he said, because she had twins at the end of the story. 'Yet they were not married,' his tobacco stained fingers accused us. 'Was it a sin, Father?' Falvey asked in a holy voice, his pen poised to inscribe the answer for posterity. Fr O'Growney scratched his head and rolled his eyes. There was nothing in Canon Law to help him, he said. 'But though it might not have been a sin, one had to admit their behaviour was sinful.' Falvey acclaimed the wisdom of this judgement by nodding his head gravely. Furthermore, pagan morality was wrong because it was the man who was punished in the end, not the woman. 'It is the woman who tempts, it is she who must suffer.' Fr O'Growney said that the end of the book, where she had twins, would never come up on the exam because the Department of Education had never embarrassed Catholic morality in thirty-five years of exams. For the same reason we skipped large passages of Euripides' *Medea* because it was a filthy play.

There was a rug on the floor of the Ritz. I didn't ask her about it. We were meeting there regularly, almost every second night. She said it was very difficult to get away from the maids' quarters because Matron was an insomniac. She was frightened of the long dark passages that led to the Ritz, but it was worth it all, she smiled. I asked her not to use perfume, because I couldn't pass it off as shaving lotion. She was pale and had circles under her eyes. I said that maybe we should make it every third night but she said definitely no. She had cigarettes and we each sat on a chamber-pot and smoked Sweet Afton. She brought four mutton chops in a napkin which she said were left over after the priests' dinner.

In the hurling-field Sandra took her toll. 'That's the third fifty you've missed in a row, you're going cross-eyed,' roared Fr Johnson in rage as he ran up and down the sideline. I played centre field for my college but the late nights showed in my reflexes and dulled my kicking instinct. 'Lie down, lie down, b'y',' he hissed at me after half-time, 'or St Fachtna's will drive us into the ground,' and his two fingers pointed down at the mucky ground. I lay down as if injured and shortly a fresh player took my position. I complained to Fr Johnson at the sideline about being run-down. 'I know,' he said out of the corner of his mouth, 'three raw eggs every morning and one at night.'

Sandra brought bagfuls of toffees, German sausage and chocolate Swiss rolls to the Ritz. We ate them in the darkness and whispered. Her father was a harness-maker in the town; it was hard on him because all the farmers were selling their horses and buying tractors. She asked about my family. I lied. I said my father was a poor fisher-man down by the sea. She said it was great to be poor, that she loved the sea, that I must miss the fish terribly and that she would bring a tin of sardines the next time. That night as I was making my way to the dormitory, I bumped into O'Connell who was coming from the toilet. I was so surprised I shone the lamp at him and asked if he had been smoking. He blew his sour breath in my face and walked away with loathing in his eyes.

Fr McKinley taught Catechism. He said that he had been to Africa, which had changed his life. He felt superior to all those people whose lives had not yet been changed. He advised us to go to Africa in order to see the light. A light malarial sweat dampened his forehead as he analysed a mortal sin for us. He held up three fingers. 'Only three little things to remember for a mortal sin: you must have grievous matter, full consent, and perfect knowledge.'

That night as our bodies tumbled about, I tossed McKinley's grisly triad in my mind. Grievous matter wrapped its limbs about my body while full consent and perfect knowledge were on a rampage.

The college chapel stank of B.O. and incense. Fr O'Shiel was giving out Communion. Seat by seat communicants were evacuated to the altar. When my seat's turn came I stayed as I was, rosary beads in hands, my lips uttering nonsense syllables. I was the only one who remained, my hunched form advertising a soul not in a state of grace. Time and again Fr O'Shiel glanced at me, our eyes entering a communion more subtle than that of any unleavened bread.

We never heard the door open, but we felt the icy torchlight pass through our naked bodies. She froze in shock and made no effort to cover herself as the light played over her small nutmeg breasts and thighs. The door closed noiselessly. It took me ages to squeeze and hug her back to awareness and then she began to shudder. I had to dress her in the darkness and lead her up the long corridor to her quarters. She was crying and talking about her job and her father, her two hands digging into my arms. I tried to comfort her, saying that forgiveness was a Christian virtue. 'What will become of us?' she whimpered as she stumbled away from me into the darkness of the sculleries.

Fr Johnson held me back at the door after Mass. The others filed past us with suitable expressions of piety. I would not be allowed to breakfast with them, he said. Instead I was to pack my bags and breakfast on my own when classes had started.

I carried my bags through the mass of bodies retreating from breakfast, my stony face and my butting suitcases forcing a path through the throng. They greeted me in silence and in awe, the worst of them clinching my sin with pious expressions, the best shambling in confusion. Falvey was smirking. I marked him down for the hurling-field. Christ, if I could only get his kidneys west of the butt of my hurley.

I had some weak tea at the bottom of the refectory, in silence. A large maid served me, a quirk distorting her face. Other ugly scullions came to look at me, their slyness stripping me of my manhood. In vain I peered into the steamy kitchen for a trace of her.

Two priests sat at the table, water, pencils, and paper in front of them. Fr Shore and Fr O'Shiel.

'This is very serious,' said Fr Shore. 'You realize that, of course.'

Fr O'Shiel stared gravely at his finger.

'No, I don't know what you're talking about,' I said.

Fr Shore was stopped in mid-flight. He looked puzzled.

Fr O'Shiel said, 'But this is monstrous.'

Fr Shore almost smiled. 'Surely you know why you are here. You have committed a most grievous offence.'

'What grievous offence?'

They both looked in consternation at each other.

'Now look here, Stack, you're a prefect and we expect a little more from our prefects. You know well why you're here.'

'Tell me then.'

'Stack, try to remember that you are scholarship material, you have a career in front of you, and we can be lenient.'

'Yes, and you haven't had a scholarship in fifteen years.' I only felt rage at myself more than at them. 'Which one of you shone the torch anyway?'

There was a pause, their grey eyes bored through me.

'Why do you ask?' said Fr O'Shiel.

'Because whoever it was had a good look and it wasn't at me he was looking.'

Fr Shore uttered a choking cry and rose to his feet, his face horribly flushed.

'This is monstrous,' he was almost crying. 'I have never been so insulted in all my life.' As he headed for the door, Fr O'Shiel stopped me, turning on me at the same time with poison in his eyes.

'Right, Stack, expulsion, out, finis. Be here at three p.m. to remove yourself to the dark nothingness whence you came.'

It was raining lightly in the town as I sauntered about. I paused near the town clock and looked up the lane at the rows of pieshops, cobblers' shops and artisan cottages. It was dark in the harness-maker's shop where a small whiskery man worked on a collar and hames with a knife. He answered my request by looking at me for a long time.

'Sandra,' he shouted hoarsely. She came out looking red-eyed, grabbed my hand and then took me into the lane. 'What did they do to you, Denis?' she asked with concern. I had seen her only once before in daylight. I didn't think she looked pretty now. 'Threw me out. What will you do?'

She twisted a piece of her blouse. 'I don't know,' she said nervously. 'My father might give me my fare for the boat.' I fingered the ten-pound note in my pocket. We promised to write.

My father came at an awful pace in the Landrover, towing the trailer.

'Did he put her up the pole, Father?'

'I beg your pardon.' Fr Shore recoiled into the chaise-longue.

'Did you put her up the pole, Dennisheen, you hoor?'

'No.'

'Are you sure?' He smelt of fresh milk and cow-dung.

'Yes.'

He turned his flushed face back on the two priests. 'What's all the fuss about so?'

Fr O'Shiel fixed him with savage eyes. 'There's a little matter of rustication.'

'What's that in the honour of Christ?' His nose was quivering with fright. They both looked at him with distaste.

'It means I've got to go home for a week,' I said.

'Can he come back again?' said my father with relief.

'Yes,' I said with finality.

As we drove up through the town my father was laughing so much his hat was falling over his eyes.

'I got Coneen on the job. He's the boy for them. All the way to Maynooth. I'm telling you he set fire to their arses.' He looked at me. 'I'm telling you I got Coneen to get you fixed up,' he said gruffly. I answered that I was grateful to Uncle Con, the Monsignor.

We went into the pub at the top of the town. As my father eased himself on to the bar-room stool he said. 'By the way, who were those two little farts I was talking to in the college?'

'Fr Shore and Fr O'Shiel.'

'Where're they from?'

'Bowermola.'

'Well, I should have known,' he said in triumph. 'Midgets from Bowermola. Nothing to eat. Goats and bogholes. By Christ, it must have been a bad year for spuds when they took that pair into the Church.' He asked me what I would have to drink and I said stout. He almost fell off the chair with surprise. 'A pint of stout,' I repeated firmly. He nodded to the barmaid. When I was half-way through my pint he began to laugh uncontrollably.

'By God, you're a terrible bastard.' He shouted at the barmaid: 'This fellow is a terrible bastard.' He opened my shirt. 'A terrible hairy bastard. What would a girl give for a feel of that?'

The barmaid said she was sure they'd give a lot, that I was very lucky because some men had chests as bare as the palms of her hand. And she displayed her open palm to everybody.

We had another drink, my father laughing every time he saw the pint in front of me. I wondered at the black power in my glass that could make my father give me such comradely looks. He moved his stool closer to me and said out of the corner of his mouth, 'What was she like, son?'

I looked at my pint and at my father's half-embarrassed, eager face.

'She had big tits,' I said.

'Sure, all scrubbers have big tits,' he said in matey confidence, clinching his wisdom with a wink. I fingered the ten-pound note in my pocket.

'I could tell you a thing or two about big tits. There was this barmaid down in Ballybunion who had half the country driven mad with her tits. Before I met your mother, of course,' he said.

I thought of her breasts, small as nutmegs in the cool air of the Ritz and I felt a cold dissatisfaction with life take hold of me. I asked my father to get going.

As we drove the long road west my father spoke of the success of the farm. Pound notes were springing up from every field of the three hundred and forty acres.

'And not one penny tax.'

And it was amazing what a farmer married to a national school-teacher could do because she didn't pay income-tax either. But the farm labourers had to pay tax. It was funny to see their faces every Friday as they headed for the pub. Farmers had been down too long and now they were coming into their own. Ireland was a paradise for farmers and there were grants for pissing crooked.

We stopped at the county boundary for another drink. My father bought a red calf from a ragged man in the yard and we put him in the trailer. 'For the freezer,' my father said. As we drove off he added with satisfaction, 'A suckey calf for sixteen and sixpence.' It was a great country and if we had more time he could have knocked another half-crown off the man.

As we drove through the mild traffic, the calf in the trailer began to be thrown about. Every time we stopped it was almost forced through the rails. I listened to it fall and low in fright.

'Yerra, he's all right back there,' my father answered me in that gruffness that passed for manliness among farmers. As we continued on I felt its fear and pain infect me in a way I would never have thought possible.

'Stop the car,' I said to my amazed father. I repeated it and he drew the car slowly to a halt. I tied the calf with ropes around its belly and neck. Then I decided the rope around its neck was too tight and I placed my coat under the rope. 'Have you gone out of your mind, b'y, your good coat around a calf?' I stood sheepishly and said it would be good for the flesh in the freezer.

After a while my father said the coat was a damn good idea and talking about freezers, he had two dozen ducks in the freezer. 'I bought them from Jackeen Breshnihan's widow. Did you know Jackeen died? Drink. How much did I pay for them? Go on, give a guess.'

'Ten shillings a duck.'

'No.'

'Eight shillings a duck.'

'You're getting warm,' was his gleeful reply.

'Two shillings a duck.'

'Jaysus Christ,' he said as if cheated, 'who's going to give you a duck for two shillings? But you're not far wrong, four and tuppence, just think of that.' It was a great country when you could get a duck for four and tuppence. 'If you have money you can do the divil himself.'

He told me that Mary Kissane was going to do medicine, that she was a lovely girl and that it was great that both she and I hit it off so well. I had taken her to a dance once; what he did not mention was that she had two hundred acres 'bounding' on our land and that she wore glasses. He stopped the car on the hill overlooking our land and we looked at the lush fields and the stumps of oak and beech that disguised the two-storey dwellings. 'This is Stack country, son. Generations of blood have gone into its soil.' A few pints always made him think of his ancestors. 'I can think of no better person than yourself to inherit it all. Myself and herself are getting on.' He grabbed me by the hair of my head and said with passion: 'Dennisheen, you're the kind of lad we want. Could you take it?'

I said yes.

'Would you think of Mary?'

I nodded my head in understanding. Tears came into his eyes.

'If you do, son, it's a straight run for both of you down to Killcash.' Killcash was our graveyard and a straight run down to it was the local euphemism for a happy life.

My mother was thin and jaundiced from spending her life tending a large Aga cooker. Her name was Eileen but my father never called her anything. When his sentences were addressed to her they always ended in a special rising infection. She sat now by the Aga and looked at me in a frightened manner.

'What did she do to you?'

My father explained that I had got involved with a slut, a real wily woman of the world, but that God and His Blessed Mother had delivered me from her clutches and that she had got what she deserved.

'What did she do to you, Denis?' she kept on whining. I ate my duck in silence, while my father told her what happy days were in store for us all. After a while he slipped out to Kirby's for a last pint. As I trudged upstairs, my mother begged me to say an Act of Contrition. 'The long one,' she said, and that I could go to Confession next morning.

The sheets were cool as I lay in bed. The walls were full of holy pictures: Mary Magdalen holding a chalice, the Little Flower with a little flower, and a huge Sacred Heart bearing the inscription that John and Eileen Stack were enrolled in the League of Eternal Prayer. I shut my eyes but I couldn't sleep. I tossed in anguish at the thought of my father in Kirby's lying about big-titted Ballybunion barmaids to a little knot of men who had ducks and calves they couldn't feed. I thought of my mother's dry bones bent above the Aga, her lips mouthing pious aspirations for her soul, for mine. I thought of the straight run down to Killcash.

The Quizmasters

I lived in an old house by the river. Except for the swish of the water and the rafters which creaked in the cold, it was a silent house. At night things moved in the weeds. In winter I stood to my ankles in the cooling snow and gazed in wonder at the beauty of my house. In summer farmers gathered with implements to cut the things that had chanced to grow, releasing their sweet quick on the dry air. They planked their misshapen faces on the fence. 'Let us kill your weeds for you,' they implored, waving billhooks and sickles in the air. I smiled with contempt at them.

I sat in my house and listened to the thistles knock at my window in a breeze, reminding me that I do not meddle, that I do no violence to this earth. This creed left my house in disarray but it is better to live in squalor with a philosophy than to be tidy and in pain.

I worked in a funny place: the Quiz School of St Patcheen. The Quizmasters were all funny too. If they saw me laugh they shook their fists in anger and scolded me. 'Shirker, layabout, get some work done.' One doesn't laugh in a funny school. There were also 325 brats in my school.

Brutus Iscariot was the headmaster; some said he was an escaped priest. He was very involved in the community. Every morning he put a 'Do Not Disturb' sign on his door and shinned down the drainpipe at the back of the school. I waited for him there one morning to discuss with him the matter of my money, which was in arrears. He came down with a thump, surprised.

'Oh, it's you, you feckless lazybones. When are you going to stop swinging the lead, pull up your socks, get off your ass and get down to the nitty gritty?'

'I've sent for some new quizzes,' I said. Then I paused for words.

Should I call my money a stipend, gratuity, or honorarium? It was always in Latin, all part of the insult. 'What about my pay?' I blurted out.

He gave me the humourless smile of the escaped priest. 'Why do Quizmasters think so much about their pay, and so little about their reward?' and he squinted slyly up to heaven. Then he was gone in a flash down the boreen to say Mass or open a dog show.

The Quizmasters never stayed out sick. Every morning they presented themselves for duty with crushing repetition. Nor did they ever interfere with the running of the school, except once in their lives: that's the day the Great Inspector himself came to visit. They say the angel of death is so busy in schools that he wears a mortar board; but he is efficient and kind to teachers. One great farewell thump in the chest, chalky hands grasp the air, before your brave pedagogue keels over to achieve the Great Horizontal. There he lies fallen until discovered by charwomen. But if the brats in their desks liked the Quizmaster, one usually went to Brutus and shouted, 'Another cardiac arrest in room 5A.' The brats were well used to the discipline of Quizmasters' funerals and their behaviour was good, for they would rather follow a Quizmaster to his grave than follow him down the grey road of the third declension.

It is easy to fill a Quizmaster's position. Take Cerberus, for instance. He was originally trained for the jail next door to St Patcheen's, but he came in the wrong gate. Brutus immediately banished him to the classroom. They say old Cerberus never knew the difference. At night he wandered through the corridors communicating with doors and locks. Brutus got most of his teachers like that, anybody who came to the door, plumbers, gravediggers, and Jehovah's Witnesses. The butcher's boy was terrified of Brutus. His latest plan was to hang the sausages on the door-knocker and run. It was also because of Brutus' little habit that no inspectors would visit the school.

All the Quizmasters had long shadows but Rigormortis beat them all. He was very thin and carried a shadow twenty-three feet long. I know because I measured it one day when he wasn't looking. When he came in in the morning his shadow was in front of him spying out the corridor, but in the evening he had to drag it all the way out into the twilight. The other Quizmasters said that Rigormortis' shadow wasn't his own but belonged to something that had died. It was bad luck to step on it. He never approached the staff-shed in the yard but took his lunch by himself in the stone corridor. There he sat erect among the Ogham stones, his bony fingers filching bread from a paper bag, masticating each bite thirty times. He was proud of his thirty mastications and resulting good health. Rigormortis had no nickname, for Rigormortis could be likened to nothing but things could be likened to Rigormortis, like Celtic crosses and Ogham stones.

Size is very important; people don't realize that. I'm always measuring things. Interruptus, the first day he came to the Quiz School on his tricycle, was all of four and a half feet. He was unusually energetic; tall Quizmasters had to be wary of him or they were chinned in the crotch. One day when we were in the queue for our free pencils and rubbers, I noticed that Interruptus, who was in front of me, came up only to the bottom button of my waistcoat. When I explained to him that he was diminishing and would shortly have to be replaced, he disagreed with me. After that Interruptus cut me dead but took to wearing large hats. Nobody likes the truth.

Neither did Sufferinjaysus. Nobody ever spoke to Sufferinjaysus when they met him in the corridors, they just grunted in sympathy. He quizzed in a room with the curtains continually drawn. Two fires heated two generations of sweaty adolescent BO and Vick. Sufferinjaysus was concerned about his health. He stood in the room with his back to the fire and tossed Euclidian cuts to the brats. We borrowed fag-ends from each other; but when I heard his Local Defence Force boots drag in the corridor I had to be wary; to this day I think he owes me three. He was at his best in a pub when he enthused about body building courses, and laughter, and sunshine in his childhood. But he was not graceful. I always say that those who are neither graceful nor elegant should be belted with porter bottles on the back of the head.

Vercingetorix was the greatest enigma of all. He was the Latin Quizmaster and was so calm and composed at all times that I was suspicious. He never did anything wrong like being sick, laughing or having a cardiac arrest. But his brothers told me his secret. Every Friday Vercingetorix covered the dining room table with copybooks to be corrected. The brothers, all six of them, bachelors, played poker by the fire. Suddenly something would happen to Vercingetorix's mind. For a split second in his week sanity took over. He would arise from the table trembling, looking strangely at the copybooks. 'I'm not a Quizmaster; I couldn't be one,' he'd say in revulsion.

'Yes you are,' the brothers would reply in unison.

'Well I deserve a good walloping so.'

Immediately the brothers would rush upon him, fetching him clouts and wallops until they brought him to the ground; while on the ground the oldest brother, who was a dwarf and had to wait his turn, would kick him in the crotch. Vercingetorix would then pass out with a delighted groan. After a while he'd pick himself up, the calmest man in Academia.

Ah, but Miss Parnassus, dear, darling Miss Parnassus. She is a born Quizmistress, quite literally. When she was seven days old her parents put chalk into her hand, and her dear little fist closed on it so tightly they couldn't feed her for days. I'm in love with Miss Parnassus. I was always asking her for chalk so that I could touch her, my little finger tarrying in her chalky palm. What a treat I say! She has a little hair on the tip of her nose that I would dearly like to play with. I was always pressing my rulers on her. I never gave rulers to anyone else. As a result I had lots and lots of them in my press, rulers of every kind, mind you. But she didn't seem to need them. I need them myself for measuring.

One day I told Miss Parnassus that I had a little house by the river in the country. She didn't seem interested. But because she is a born Quizmistress I knew she would relent when I told her about my invention for correcting essays. We went out on a spring day and walked in pedagogical communion by the river banks, she remarking on how gaily the little verbs twittered in their conjugations, while I pointed out the tidy nests the nouns built in their declensions.

My little house stood out proud from its greenery. Her face began to harden as she picked her way through my weeds. She almost balked at the briars at the front door. I took my Miss Parnassus into my house, a real live woman in my house. I almost felt weak. I hastened to her needs, dusting chairs for her, putting on the kettle, rinsing a cup for her and cushing the flies out the window.

She stood in the middle of the floor, her eyes narrowing at the disarray of my parlour. I sat at her feet and gaped up at her, my eyes imploring some kindness.

'Why don't you kill those filthy weeds?' she asked. I lectured her on labels, pointing out that weeds were careless flowers, that the word weed was divisive and suggestive of a rank (no pun) that did not exist, that I preferred the word 'plant' for all green things.

'Well, why don't you clean up this?' she said, sweeping her hand in contempt at my little disarray. I looked about me and said that the things in my environment could depend on me not to destroy them. While the iron was hot I showed her my invention. From a purple box I took out four rubber stamps. On each was written respectively, 'Very good', 'Very bad', 'Not so good', 'Not so bad'.

I grabbed a bundle of copies that had been in the corner for years and attacked them with the rubber stamps, each correction raising a cloud of dust.

'This is revolutionary,' I said with excitement and Miss Parnassus began to cough. In no time at all I despatched forty of the wretched things back into the corner. But poor Miss Parnassus, she was still coughing and her eyes were red. She said she had flu and had to go. I escorted her tenderly to the door.

The next day I went to Miss Parnassus' room and with a big smile asked her for chalk. She said she had none. I retreated in consternation to my own roomful of brats. There I did a lot of thinking. I decided that if I were to be successful I would have to rearrange my furnishings, do some dusting perhaps.

That evening I wandered through the rooms of my house, noting the soiled shirts, the coffee stains, the cigarette ash, old shoes and dirty socks, beds that had never been made, broken delph and mildew. It was no use, I could not raise my hand against them.

So it went for days, reflecting, contemplating, vacillating, round and round my head went in agonizing circularity.

It happened on Friday. As soon as I opened the door I smelt it: floor polish. I opened my eyes wide at the shining hall. I inched my way in, in dread. All the floors shone like plates, walls scrubbed down, furniture polished and arranged in a pleasing fashion, neat rows of shining delph on the dresser, and the bathroom smelt of flowers. But I nearly lost my mind when I saw the bed. White starched sheets, pillows puffed out with pride, eiderdown arranged artistically. I took one jump and landed in the middle of it, yelping with joy, burying my face in the white coolness of the sheets. It was like an iced cake and I could have eaten it. I jumped and frolicked and tossed my pyjamas in the air. It brought me back to my childhood and the smell of the bread in the oven. Suddenly I got up and looked about me. Then I pranced around the house examining doors and windows. Everything was intact.

I have a host of good friends who would only be too willing to do all this in lieu of the many kindnesses which it is my nature to perform, but after a second glance I realized that this had been done by a woman. Bang went the friends theory. It was of course Miss Parnassus. Yes, I decided, this was performed out of love.

Next day I didn't ask her for any chalk. It is always better to let these things happen naturally. I stayed in my room smiling knowingly and listening for her dainty walk in the corridor. The brats were sniggering, they were quick to catch on to something. I don't mind, in love one can be tolerant. I even promised them new quizzes.

A few days later she had been there again. There were two laundry bags in the bathroom with labels attached to them, 'Coloureds', 'Whites'. In the kitchen delph was laid out for a meal. I was very pleased with her work, and I yelped with lonesome glee. I went on my now accustomed pilgrimage through the rooms, sniffing, and feeling, and peering at myself in mirrors. Then I noticed my whiskey. With great misgivings I extracted a ruler from my pocket and measured. I was right, there were about four half ones missing. I slept very poorly that night for I would not be pleased with a tippling woman for a wife.

On the following Monday I rushed home on my bicycle without even bothering to fasten the clips on my trousers. More whiskey was gone and some food. I didn't mind about the food. Then I saw a note on the mantelpiece, 'Use the ashtrays please'. She was so right in a way. I was proud of the house, I was pleased with her work, but the whiskey was another matter. I decided to go to her the following day and have it out with her.

But alas, next day old Semper Virens, the Irish Quizmaster, achieved the Great Horizontal in the middle of the past subjunctive.

He had been sitting so long in his oaken rostrum that bark encased his knees. It had been decided that should he take root he should be cut down and made into rulers, a commodity in sore supply in my school. But no plans were ready. As they took old Semper Virens out through the hall in his coffin, Brutus Iscariot was livid with rage.

'Jesus Christ, what a day to get a hea– . . . a cardiac arrest. Six weeks to the Leaving Certificate; where will it all end?' Only Semper Virens knew. Brutus had to give us all a half day and both brats and Quizmasters ran for the gate in high glee.

I went early to the house and that's how I discovered it all. There was a man in my kitchen with an apron on; he was washing dishes by the sink and hummed idly to himself. He didn't even look up.

'Who on earth are you and what are you doing in my house?' I was outraged. He had an unusual calmness about him which I found cheeky. His eyes were cold and expressionless. He never answered, just continued to hum in an empty fashion.

'Where did you get the key to come into my house?' I said, not without anger.

'I didn't come in,' he said, 'I was here always.'

'Now, now,' I said, 'I'll have none of that, not in my house.' I was quite firm, a quality I have learned from my profession.

'Come,' he said peremptorily. I followed him out to the hallway. 'Look,' he said and he pointed up at the attic trap door. It was open, and I gazed up at the square darkness.

'I never saw that before. You came down from there you say?'

'Yes, I have been there always, it's quite a nice place really.'

I found a step-ladder and climbed up. I stuck my head into that inky blackness and I immediately felt a strange calm.

'I can't see anything,' I said. 'It's very dark.'

'You don't have to see anything, that's why I'm up there. It's also quiet and peaceful and nobody bothers you.'

'I suppose you're right. Is it dry?'

'As dry as a haystack. There's great shelter up there. There's wood, felt, and slate between you and the weather.'

'How do you spend your time up there?'

'In thought.'

'You're right too. I'm worn out from thought myself, but it's great isn't it?'

I came down and we went to the kitchen. I filled out whiskey for myself as I usually do in company. I think he looked rather perturbed about the whiskey, or maybe it was my feet.

'I'd appreciate it if you wouldn't put your feet on the table.'

I did as he said.

'I'd like you to know that you're doing a grand job here, and I'm very grateful.'

'You needn't be grateful but be careful.' And he danced off around the house, flicking pictures and ornaments with a rag.

'You have a nice house,' he called from the hallway. 'We both have,' I shouted back, but I heard the attic trap door bang. I was alone again. I walked around my little palace a few times, as proud as an archdeacon. It was as clean as the chalice. I made tea and called up to him but he didn't answer. I have noticed that people of great depth are like that. I drank my tea and watched my purple thistles dance in the breeze. Company is a great thing.

Next day I went into Miss Parnassus' room. She charmed me with a gorgeous blush. She spoke crossly to me but I know that a good Quizmistress must be cross. I pressed some rulers on her but she refused. Then I spoke to her out of the side of my mouth about a certain house, telling her (and I winked at her) that it was a palace. The brats began to snigger and Miss Parnassus began to write on the blackboard. I shrugged at the brats and left the room.

I sat alone in the kitchen. After a while the man from the rafters alighted. He examined the house and I am proud to say it was perfect. While he helped himself to my whiskey I complained about Miss Parnassus.

'Have patience, man, you'll see her in this house yet.' He said it with such conviction that it fired my soul. I was getting fond of a man who could give such good advice.

For days I sat in my quizroom listening for her dainty walk in the corridor, knowing that each step brought her closer to me.

'What kind of work do you do?' he said one day to me. I explained about the Quiz School. But he wanted details. I explained about the importance of working at a higher level than the brats. He immediately stood on an old orange case.

'Like this?'

I nodded. Then I explained about the quiz book in the Quizmaster's hand, and the quizzes.

'What sort of quizzes?'

'Oh,' I said, 'the usual thing: who made the world. Depths of rivers, tombstones and anything generally about long ago.' He wanted to know what one did if they didn't answer.

'Correct them,' I said.

'How?'

'Roar,' I answered. The man from the rafters roared suddenly and gave me quite a fright.

'Is that all?' he asked. I mentioned the importance of learning to balance copybooks on the carrier of one's bicycle, of having at least three good jokes and of the folly of joining a pension scheme.

'Sure any old fool could do that,' he said. I hung my head with shame for I knew he spoke the truth, but my loyalty to the profession would not allow me to admit it.

On another occasion he said to me when he had alighted beside me, 'It grieves me to see a man of your potential and undoubted talents slaving your life away day in, day out.'

The truth of the statement shocked me. I got up on unsteady feet and grasped his hand. 'You are a true friend.' His hand was cold.

'Isn't it time you took a day off?'

'It certainly is, but what excuse could I have?'

'Sick.'

'Can't go sick. It's not permitted.'

'How about a heart attack?'

'You may only have one cardiac arrest. He who has the second one is never forgiven.

We were silent for some time. Suddenly he slapped his hands together.

'I have it: you stay here and I will go in your place.' It was a brilliant idea but it was dangerous.

'They'd be quick to catch on to something like that where I work. You'd be recognized.'

'How would I? They don't know me. Anyway, I'm good with disguises.' I was uncomfortable.

'I'd be missed, I think.'

'Maybe not, try it. Just think of it, you could take a week given over to thought. Furthermore, I invite you to go the attic and really contemplate.'

That did it.

'Really, you wouldn't mind?'

'Certainly not, you are more than welcome.'

I was dying for a go at the attic; for too long I had been observing the man from the rafters and marvelling at what an attic could do for a man. With a mixture of foreboding and excitement I agreed, and we went to bed.

The sun was hardly up when the commotion in the kitchen awakened me; I trotted out in my bare feet. There he was on his knees with my rubber stamps, giving the copybooks hell.

'What's going on?'

'Correcting.'

'They've been there for years, some of those guys are dead.'

'It doesn't matter,' he said, 'their parents might like a souvenir. Anyway, the place has to be cleared.'

I looked down at the battered, dogeared copies, stained with beer and coffee on the outside, and inside a cemetery of useless information.

At eight-thirty he tottered to the door with copies and piled them on the carrier of my bike. As he was about to mount he called out to me, 'By the way, what's your name?'

'Anthropos, Mr Anthropos,' I shouted back as I watched him sway away to work. I had misgivings, but I felt exhilarated at the prospect of the attic.

I stuck my head through the square darkness of the trap and entered upon the black peace of freedom from the flesh. I lay on his rug and felt the fears and regrets and terrors of work rise off my bones as a fine dust and float away into the unknown abyss of the attic. I developed a theory about attics and the wonderful way that wood, felt and slate protected a body from the hostile vibrations that beset ordinary rooms.

The door-bang signalled me to emerge from that sweet well of release and to enter the world of foolish men again. I shoved my head down to welcome the man back but he was so busy with armfuls of copies that he didn't notice me. I alighted full of wonder at the world again and I followed him into the room.

'Well, how did the day go?' I said as I picked up a fistful of copies and flung them into the corner as is my wont. The man from the rafters grew very flustered at this and ran to the corner to retrieve them. He restacked them again. The copies were new and had freshly inked work on them.

'Got to keep the place tidy,' he said.

'Anybody say anything to you today?'

'No.'

'Anybody remark anything peculiar?'

'No. Have you not made tea yet?' He was disgruntled. He was so right to mention it.

During tea we had a conversation.

'Did Brutus Iscariot see you?'

'Yes.'

'I had a bloody great spiritual day in the attic.'

'Good, that's the place to be, the attic.'

'I feel marvellous after it, never had to lift my hand all day.'

'There you are, not a tap to do and all day to do it.'

'Oh yes, and the peace of it all.'

We had a great conversation like that. I like the bit of company. He offered me the attic for the night. I gladly accepted.

When he came in the following evening, he still bustled about with more copies.

'What's this, I say,' he said, 'no beds made and no tea.' While I did the necessary housework he corrected furiously with my invention. By sheer chance I happened to see one of the copies. 'Good Lord,' I said, 'what are you doing with Rigormortis' copies here?'

'I'm just giving my friend Mr Rigormortis a helping hand,' he answered in a threatening manner.

I went through more of them. 'And Sufferinjaysus and Interruptus? Well I declare, their copies processed by my invention. I'm not at all pleased.'

He looked at me with that cool cheeky look of his. 'Rest assured that both Quiz School and Quizmasters are indebted to you for your invention.' This had a mollifying effect on me.

That night I had an attic dream; I dreamt that cold porridge was being flung into my eyes. And all the next day uneasy thoughts began to press in on my meditation. I stopped him at the door that evening and checked through his copybooks. My suspicions were correct: he had got to Miss Parnassus. I took his wretched copies and scattered them evenly throughout the house.

'Double crosser,' I roared at him. 'And I thought you were my friend.' I shook the step-ladder in anger. I know I look very terrible in a rage. He crept quietly up into the attic and I pulled the step-ladder away.

'And stay up there from now on. I'm going to work tomorrow.'

He stuck his head down and looked dissatisfied. 'But I must go to work tomorrow or I will be accused of being sick.' I couldn't argue with a man whose face was upside-down.

I was up early, feet washed, shoes polished and all that. I was very pleased as I went into the staff-shed that morning; I like to assert myself. All Quizmasters were along the wall as usual. Brutus Iscariot detached himself from the noticeboard and came over to me.

'Well, my good man, and what can I do for you?'

'Nothing, I'm going to take my class.'

'You must be mistaken, you are not known here.'

'I'm Anthropos.' There was a dryness in my mouth.

'Where is Mr Anthropos this morning?' he addressed the Quizmasters.

They all surrounded me, their long shadows falling all around me like the spokes of a wheel.

'He must be sick, he's working too hard,' said Sufferinjaysus.

'Yes, I agree,' yelped Miss Parnassus.

'I'm Anthropos,' I said with the wail of a man betrayed.

'Liar, impostor, actor,' they roared as they pointed their chalky fingers at me. I backed away from these monsters and fled down the steps. I fled along the lanes through the countryside in terror for I felt the shadow of Rigormortis in my rear.

I rushed in the open doorway of my house so fast that I was up the step-ladder and encapsulated in my attic by the man in the rafters before I realized where I was.

'And stay up there,' he shouted after me. 'I'm late already as it is,' and he trotted off to work. I was so jaded from my experience that I never said a word. It took a whole day of meditation for me to regain my composure.

Towards evening as I levitated around the rafters, I heard the screech of metal on stone. Someone was edging a scythe, backwards and forwards went the motion, its sound filling the attic with foreboding. Then I listened in horror to the dry shearing of its blade as it set my plants in a swathe, scattering the green force of their lives on the evening air. I lay back and felt my courage ebb further with each vicious swipe.

He had company in the house. I like company, but this was a woman. I heard their low talk and sudden laughter. The nudges, the knowing winks and the slyness, I could imagine. I groped around the rafters until I found a chink. I put my eye to it. Red hot pokers stabbed my brain; Miss Parnassus was on the sofa. But that wasn't all; flesh, white flesh, the whiteness of sheltered modesty there in carnal display. Oh, the filth of it and the poison of such sinful undertakings. Just anger swept out from my soul and terrible was the sound of my grinding teeth. I'm a terror in a rage. Like Samson I gripped the rafters and could have brought the house down upon their lusting bodies were it not that Mr Anthropos wants no noise from the attic. I lay back and had to listen to their delight while they shared each other's privacy until my sleep released me.

Last night I knocked on the trap-door. After a while he unlocked it and stuck his head up.

'Could I have a drink of water please, sir, it's dry up here.'

He considered this for some time.

'Will you want to make your wee-wee after it?'

'Oh no, sir, that only happens after two drinks of water.'

'Very well,' and he fetched me a nice cool drink.

'I'm rather pleased with your housework, although I would suggest greater effort in the culinary area,' he said.

'Right, sir. You just leave that to me,' I said. 'By the way, sir, when do we have a little chat again? I rather like a little chat.'

He paused to think. 'After tea tomorrow then, if everything is in order.'

I thanked him and he locked the trap-door.

Mr Anthropos is like that, straight if you are straight with him. I help a little now and then but in the attic I am king. Up here I never have to lift a hand, and himself waits on me hand and foot. Up here I have great peace, as I listen to the woodworm burrow the dry seconds of their lives away.

The Man Who Stepped on His Soul

There is a beach in Kerry, long and straight as a knife, clean as a chalice, and the first men that gazed upon it sighed, and called it Lonely Banna Strand. Press a shell to your ear and hear its loneliness, windswept and timeless down by an endless sea. Far out where all is still, sunlight drops through the tall green gloom of the ocean, but inshore land and wave commemorate each other with dry satisfying sand. And when the wind blows, it tosses seagulls far inland beyond the trees, beyond the fields, beyond the hills; or wilder still, it funnels sand through the keyholes of distant homes, and the surf booms out across the county reminding the old of forgotten things, haunting the young with the triumph of days to come. But its fury is the fury of mindless things and in such fury only do we find the stillness of true peace.

It wasn't for nothing it was called Lonely Banna Strand, said Tom Mullins to himself, as he cycled from his monastery westwards to the sea. He watched the fuzzy line of sandhills hop, step, and jump southward to Sliabh Mish mountains. But why do the people of Kerry now call it Banna Beach? They had already lost one language without a trace of culture shock. They would gladly lose another if they got half a chance. The word strand stood for loneliness and the washed vacancy of ocean margins; beach on the other hand brought to mind barbecues, broken bottles and unwanted human commotion. A full year now he had been in the Black Monastery of Doon, and his opinion of Kerry people had grown thin. Culture had no meaning for them, nothing worried them except pub closing times, and where was the crack. In a group they reminded him of empty

Coke bottles rattling together.

These spiteful observations eased the rheumatic hip enough for him to dismount and walk a little. It was the first few days of April and there wasn't enough snow on Sliabh Mish to satisfy a robin on a Christmas postcard. It was a day as frail as the spindrift, and although cold, there was enough sunlight to tempt one to be adventurous with clothes. He loosened his Roman collar with a finger.

It was going to be a great geographical day, for geographer he was at heart and thus coveted nature's wilderness. Today, Banna Strand would be his Gobi Desert, tomorrow the bog of Lyracrumpane would be his Okavango Swamps. He was a man who enjoyed the mystical unity of rock, tree and river, and though the geography of Ireland pleased him, it was too equable and lacked the passion of the extreme. That was why he was so devoted to all those *National Geographics* that were piled under his bed. Once a month Season Finlay, the Brother Superior, would toss the yellow magazine on the table in front of Mullins, always when there was company about. He had done it yesterday.

'I see the subscription is up again,' his tone a mixture of censure and threat.

'Beauty never comes cheap,' Mullins had replied.

'There's a geographical magazine produced in England which is much cheaper and more scientific, I believe,' the Superior offered.

'It's not for the science that I read it.'

'What for then?' Finlay's face grew a disfiguring leer and his fat eyes winked little signals at the rest of the group.

Mullins ignored the spite. After all, had he not taken a vow of humility, which had to earn its keep. He could hardly tell the company that the full-colour magazine primed his youthful soul for journeys to the bottom of the Marianas Trench, or maybe in a balloon all the way to La Paz. And of late, as the grey winds of middle age blew all about him all the more, he had taken refuge in long-lining off the Grand Banks, or on cold days he accompanied Van der Post to the centre of the Kalahari Desert.

'You must have quite a lot gathered by now,' added the Superior.

'Yes – quite a lot.'

He had in fact 323 Nat. Geog. to be exact under his bed. There was room only for 120 more. By that time he would be fifty years of age. It was as good a way as any for marking time on this earth, being informed regularly by post that another month had passed.

'Why do you keep them? Why not give them to the poor and the needy?' asked Finlay.

'I like to reread them from time to time,' he answered. Finlay had drawn himself up to his full height and had said with a smile, 'I have never in my life had to reread a book,' and he walked away through the refectory.

Mullins left the tar road, and, leaving his bike against a rotting boat, made his way out through the dunes, silently like an actor through the wings out onto a sunlit stage. One glance up and down was enough – *tabula rasa* – Banna Strand was all his, not a footprint in sight. Seeing other people's footprints on his strand was as distasteful as reading other people's letters.

Well, he was going to have a fine Gobi-Desert day. He felt as joyous as Marco Polo did the first day he set foot in it. Mullins eyed the imposing Altai mountains to the east, then took another bearing from the Nan Shan mountains to the south. You had to do that sort of thing for you could get lost easily in a desert – like the sea – and for that reason men who loved the deserts also loved the sea. With his shoe he nudged the sand. Dinosaur eggs had been discovered here once. But he wouldn't dig for them today. He looked about for his favourite Gobi mammal, the Mongolian wild ass. Not a sign – pity – for it was great to watch them doing 45 miles per hour in and out of the dunes. Down he strolled through the middle of his desert, whistling a gay tune for there are great acoustics in a desert. The people of the world did not understand their deserts, especially geographers, who quite frequently left them as blank spaces on their maps, simply because they lacked roads and towns and data on wheat production. No, deserts were cosy corners in Space, in Time, where man could empty his mind of spite, and listen to it trickle through the silent dunes for ever.

He came to a stream. Was it the Orhon or the Nank Fat? It didn't matter. He took off his shoes and stockings and rolled up his trousers. With a shoe in each hand, he dashed across the stream, but it was so numbing he almost fell in the middle. He raced out to the other side and danced on the lukewarm sand. Then he dried himself with a large white handkerchief. Suddenly he looked up – the Gobi had vanished.

He strolled to the water's edge, but had to retreat from the waves' long fetch. There was something very satisfying in the way they pounded the strand, the way they hung for a second like walls of glass with bits of seaweed trapped in them before they shattered to smithereens for ever; but spindrift began to fly and he stuck to the centre of the strand where the sand was just right for footprints. Crunch – crunch – crunch, his black polished shoes bit the sand setting up a tempo that had satisfied man since the beginning of time. He glanced behind him as he walked on and he saw the way his footprints careered about. They followed him – they were loyal. He stopped. They were about the only thing that would ever follow him in this life, each print punctuating his aloneness. But footprints would never keep the wind off your back. It must be wonderful to have a family, to have children – they'd warm your back, especially that little patch between the shoulder blades. Ah but, was he not one of the Cold Backs of the Monastery of Doon. He walked on and pondered good humouredly if they had sent him to Doon because it rhymed with doom.

But all of this was not satisfactory. Geography had escaped – introversion had arrived. Going in search of self was useless because self in its own good time came after you with a vengeance. Suddenly he saw something move. The landscape was changing, he was no longer alone. Somebody was heading down the strand towards him, spoiling things for him. He was niggardly about his wildernesses. He was about to turn for home when something about the approaching person made him pause. It was a woman, her hands waving at him as she stumbled along the base of the dunes. She fell and did not get up. Brother Mullins settled his hat on his head and headed off at a trot towards her. When he came up to her she was on her hands and knees gasping for breath, her blonde hair caging her face to the ground.

'Are you alright, something wrong?'

She raised her head still gasping, she was about thirty-five. She pointed back along the dunes.

'My husband,' she gasped, 'he's dying back there, he keeps shouting for a priest, will you go back to him, Father, I can't budge another step.'

She was American, he was sure of that. And he wasn't budging either, he was doubly sure of that.

'I regret to inform you, Madam, that I am not a priest.'

His tone was quite sharp – sharpness was respected. Woe to the meek – they did not inherit the earth. She looked open-mouthed at him.

'Aren't you a clergymen?'

'It's not a term I use. I am, madam, a member of the order of Christian Brothers. Brothers do not have confessional faculties. If you require a priest you will get one in the church of Tineel, some distance from here.'

'I don't give a damn what you are. Go back to my husband please, please he's dying, anybody will do.'

He was about to point out to her that he wasn't anybody either, but the helplessness, the pleading and the fear made him cancel his words.

'O.K.,' he said, and he set off along her set of prints without adding what was on the tip of his tongue – as long as there's no more of this priest business. For Mullins had a fierce pride and he was tired of being mistaken by people everywhere for a priest; brothers dressed exactly the same, except that their Roman collars were half an inch thinner than priests'. When people discovered their mistake they had to revise their opinion of you – and it was in this revision that all the damage was done right before your eyes. You had to stop them fast to reduce the extent of the revision.

'I am not a priest, I'm only a brother.' Only – may God deliver only the good. And then they said, 'Ah well, sure a brother is almost as good as a priest.' That *almost* was reductive, very. People couldn't cope with the pressure of readjustment. 'Oh well, sure everybody has to be something.' It was enough to make one want to join the Franciscans. Priests – he hated their seed and breed.

The woman was struggling along behind him.

'How about a doctor?' he shouted back.

'Too late,' she gasped, 'he's on a drug, Lysembuthol, if that doesn't work forget it.'

They pressed on. His left ear was exposed to the sea breeze and his earhole filled with sand. But his obsession with priests wouldn't let him alone. There had been that occasion in Salthill years ago

when two priests in a car had drawn up at the kerb and said 'Would
you like a lift, Father?' He had unwound his scarf and shown them
his collar. 'Well would you like a lift anyway?' He had refused with
a smile. As their car had pulled away he had envied them their
worldliness, their car, their freedom, the fact that they didn't have
a vow of poverty as he had. No, he didn't hate priests, it was just that
they reminded him that he may have followed the wrong track in
life.

Talking about tracks, they were running out of them in the dunes
– lost. He waited and watched her try to climb a steep path up to
him. She failed and looked helplessly at him. He took her hand and
he instantly liked the sensation of her cold fingers being warmed in
his fist. So much so he was slow to relinquish it.

'I'm lost,' she said.

'Must be this way,' he said, and they trotted off again.

Suddenly they were there; a perfect sandy crater and a man of
about fifty prostrate, gasping, eyes staring at the clouds that flung
their shadows recklessly at the dunes. His blue cheeks matched the
blue of his shirt. A red polka-dot bow-tie moved to the rhythm of his
gasping, flecks of foam clinging to a small moustache. This man's
number is up, Mullins said to himself as he went on one knee beside
him. The man tried to raise himself on his elbow and say something,
but the woman pressed him back gently, placing her handbag under
his head.

'Take it easy Sean, everything is going to be alright, we have got
ourselves some help.'

She loosened his shirt and dusted the sand from it. Mullins had to
make room for her and as he did his shadow fell across the man's
face, and as it did the man's eyes fastened on the clerical collar.

'Father,' he gasped, 'I'm bunched – must make my Confession
fast. Haven't been a good boy you know, Mass, Communion and
that sort of thing.'

His hand clawed at Mullins' coat for assurance that deathbed
confessions would put his soul in the black again.

'I regret very much, my good man, that I'm not in a position to
hear your Confession or give you absolution.'

Mullins felt satisfaction in the words which were delivered with
the tiniest bit of spite for good measure; that would teach him not to

call him Father.

'Still I appreciate your condition and I would very much like to –'

The man grabbed him by the lapel and almost pulled him down on top of him.

'For God's sake, you don't have to be a bishop – it's only a piddling Confession – a bit of a blessing and everything is just bully, real bully, right?'

'Right,' said Mullins instinctively, because he couldn't refuse the pleading in the woman's eyes, and he didn't like violence either.

No sooner had he said the word than the man was off cutting through his Confession, 'Bless me, Father, for I have sinned,' followed by a rattle of familiar cliches.

Mullins almost broke out in a sweat. This was undoubtedly the worst position he had ever been in.

'I killed somebody.'

The man waited for a reaction from the priest. Mullins stared in fright at him, this was it, he was going to get up and run, he wasn't getting involved in that sort of thing.

'In the Arctic,' said the man.

The word Arctic made Mullins pause.

'I never touched the creature but I still killed him – I'll tell you about it.'

Mullins nodded.

'We were off Baffin Island in a big trawler out of Halifax, hunting halibut, but we were too far north and too close to Greenland. The winter was closing in and that damned williwaw was blowing. But we were too greedy. Instead of heading south and running, we edged north. Strike halibut and you can spend a couple of months in Mexico. But the weather hardened.'

'How far north were you? Melville?'

The man looked strangely at Mullins.

'No,' he said, about 75° North, near a peninsula called Urumsuak, I think.'

Mullins had forgotten the confession – now he was turning pages of the frozen North with full colour photography.

'Well, we struck halibut alright, but the rigging froze and we went top heavy and the strain blew the bloody boiler on us. Myself and four others barely made it to the Greenland coast – ice everywhere.

We knew our number was up but still we pressed along the edge of the pack.'

'What temperature?'

The man squinted oddly.

'Easily forty below.'

'That's celsius of course.'

The man's brow puckered, for he didn't know that he was now a talking *National Geographic*.

'There was no sun at noon, just a glimmer enough to see the polar bear. That scared us – we had no gun. That's when you know how yellow you are. Petrov, the Russian, had no gloves. His fingers turned to charcoal. He was a gonner.'

'I know,' said Mullins – see Nat. Geog. P.864, No. 6, Vol. CXIV.

'We watched his soul leak out of his eyes and his breath go spare, as we left him on a hunk of ice. Some other fella fell into a lead and never surfaced. Shortly after that we came on a small Eskimo igloo. We could have danced. He was an old hunter and we all huddled in. It was warm, it was shelter. But he had a child about a year old wrapped in a bearskin. Never could figure out how the child got there. These old Eskimos are as odd as hell, often take off for a week with a child for company. Well there was very little light the next day either but towards evening we saw rigging lights out in the bay. This must have been the last trawler on the coast. It was our last chance or we'd go like Petrov. Well, the Eskimo had this fibre-glass boat – they don't have kayaks anymore – but he wouldn't take us out. Schumacher, the mate, said we were due for a black blizzard and the trawler would skip before it. But the Eskimo wouldn't budge – he kept pointing at the little child. He refused money. Schumacher began to shout. The Eskimo got worried and pulled an old gun on us – there was a struggle, a shot, and the old guy dropped.'

'Dead?'

'Like a stone.'

He drew two deep breaths, his chest pumping up and down.

'You see the poor old devil felt the child would die if anything happened to himself. Anyway Eskimos don't trust whites.'

'I see their point.'

'Anyway, that was an accident. Outside the igloo Schumacher

said fog was coming. Up there, fog is the angel of death. We cut the heels off each other racing for the boat. We paddled like mad to the trawler. About fifty yards out we heard the child cry. We had forgotten, we stopped paddling, then we heard it again. Slowly and silently we paddled on and the wail of that child never left the stern of the boat. The trawler captain was outraged when he saw us. He had no room for us but he had no choice. When I mentioned the child to him he almost stabbed me with the marlin-spike.'

He scttled himself on the sand again, eyes as bloodshot as the setting sun.

'The cry, Father, of that child has followed me down the years.' He paused. 'And that's about it, I killed a child, that's my confession.' A note of self-pity came into his words. 'I've paid for it I tell you, year after year of bad luck, bad health, I've been dogged, I've paid for it in this life, I'm damned if I'm going to pay for it also in the next. Now be a good man and tell me you understand.'

Mullins didn't understand at all. His mind was a big windy space, and if the things that should be in his mind were there, it's not in Banna he'd be now, but living with the gauchos of the Pampas, or exploring the headwaters of the Rio Negro. But there was just this space there and the sea breeze whistling through.

'I suppose', Mullins said, 'that the child didn't last too long.'

'No, a couple of days, I'd say, hunger and cold.'

'Tell me, did you think of blocking up the entrance?'

'No,' the man looked startled.

'Anything could have got in then.'

The man held his gaze for a moment, then his head fell back again.

'Christ!' was all he said.

'Look,' said Mullins, 'what you did was not noble but the circumstances are unusual. You are contrite and as you say you have suffered. God, any God, would understand. You are forgiven, I'm sure.'

'Fine, Father, fine, but just to be on the safe side give me absolution.'

'That's something I can't do for you, son.'

'Why not?'

'I'm not a priest.'

'You're not a priest!' He was turning an ugly purple again.

'Yes, you see I'm a Christian Brother.'

He was up on one elbow again, the line of his mouth twisted into an S hook.

'Jesus, he's only a Brother.'

He looked about him at the world with eyes that would drive nails into the wall. He fell back again on the sand.

'What a joke, confessed to a Brother, that's it then, my tune is played, the dance is over.'

The woman moved in from her discreet distance, concern in her voice.

'Take it easy Sean, it doesn't matter one way or the other.'

'Look,' said Mullins in desperation, 'I'll do something which is every bit as good as absolution.'

'What's that?'

'The Act of Contrition. Repeat after me, Oh my God, I'm heartily sorry for having offended thee – '.

The man was up like a shot.

'You can shove your contrition up your ass. I know what this is now.' He was screaming. 'This is vengeance planned by God. Oh God, you're a cute hoor, all these years you were waiting to get me. And now you have me shanghaied in Banna, miles from nowhere and no absolution. You left me without children, that wasn't enough, now you want me to burn for eternity.'

His face constricted and he fell back. His wife moved fast.

'Attack, attack,' she hissed, 'he's got another attack.' She felt his pulse. 'Nothing,' she said.

She placed her ear over his heart, her blonde hair pouring over his blue shirt. Nice colour scheme, Mullins thought. The wind had gathered a drop at the tip of his nose, and he felt it would be inopportune to wipe it.

'Can you do mouth-to-mouth?' She noticed the disgust on his face. 'O.K.,' she said, 'strike him on the chest with your fist when I tell you.'

Mullins prepared himself over the body and rolled up his sleeve. The hair covered the head and chest again. Mullins was ashamed that he did not feel an ounce of pity, his own predicament had cancelled it.

'Now!'

Mullins gave the chest a small punch.

'Harder!'

He punched him harder again and again, so much that it hurt his hand.

'Anything doing?' he asked.

She shook her head. They both knew he was dead, heading down through the Milky Way, going God knows where. Still they kept it up, blow, punch, blow, punch. From time to time sand pelted them from the crests of the dunes, but she brushed every grain off the shirt. She was pale, he noticed, but calm, and those blue eyes that couldn't have hidden a thought. Unsly eyes were rare. Still, he didn't want her looking straight at him, for she gave him the flutters and he wanted to keep it dark.

'He's gone,' she said simply, sitting back on her heels.

'Maybe we should get a doctor.'

'He's gone, I said, I'm a nurse.'

'Maybe we should get a priest.'

'Is he going to make him sit up and walk?'

He didn't reply – in the circumstances it was a ridiculous suggestion.

'I need to close his eyes, have you got some coins?'

He fished and gave her two pennies. She did it with care, pulling down the blinds on the eye-shaped world of Sean somebody, who now looked up at the clouds with a harp and hen with her chicks.

'These are awfully big pennies,' she said.

'Next month we are going decimal and they will be much smaller.' Yes, everything he said was ridiculous. 'Shouldn't we do something?' he offered.

'Like what?'

'I don't know.'

She sighed. 'I knew this was going to happen. It was only a question of where.' She looked about her. 'I suppose this is as good as any, the sea, the sand, the cleanliness of it all.' Her eyes misted over and a tear squeezed out of an eye. 'What was all that about a while ago?'

'What?'

'The anger, the fear.'

'That, madam, was the fear of God.'

She pursed her lips and nodded. 'Fear and terror. Any trace of love in this land?' She took the dead man's hand in hers and twirled the ring on his finger, then pressed it to her cheek. 'Fifteen years married and all that time he gave me respect, good nature, humour, yeah, heart and soul. But three weeks ago we landed in Ireland – his homeland – and he changes overnight – sort of a cloud came down on him – worried about his mother, his family, his childhood. We visited all those broken-down cabins on that mountain there,' she indicated Sliabh Mish, 'it was like leading a frightened child through the dark. I'm sure there must also be love in this land.'

Mullins felt trapped again, trapped in a drama without a script. Why ask me about love, lady, love is a snow-capped mountain in the distance that everybody has climbed but me, love is a word you use to win an argument, to lose an argument, to win someone, to lose someone, love was a word to give yourself stature or to diminish someone else, it was the most common word in the spiritual writings of Rodriguez, all over Sunday sermons, evening devotions, nightly prayers – love is luck, something other people have, love was as common as ghosts – he had seen neither.

She was shivering. He took off his black overcoat and draped it around her shoulders.

'You don't have to do that, now you'll be cold.'

He was but he didn't care.

'Where are you going now?' he asked.

'Back to the Napa Valley, California, with Sean. Where will you go?'

'Back to the monastery, Vespers. They're prayers.'

'It must be lonely in a monastery.'

Sure, it was, so lonely sometimes he bit into his prayer book. Teeth marks everywhere.

'No, not really,' he said, 'there is great solace in prayer.' Liar, you might as well be reciting eeny, meeny, miney, mo. Tell her now, tell her the truth, you've never told anyone. Think of the relief. Sigh, and say it, be a man.

'It is refreshing to hear that,' she said. 'I'm glad that human nature has so many resources. What do they call you, your name I mean?'

Tom, you fool, say Tom. To hear her say Tom once would be better than all the yellow rubbish you have under the bed, out with it.

'Brother is the correct form of address.'

'Brother.' She said it matter of factly.

It sounded like two sods falling on his coffin. There was a long silence between them. She looked so small in his overcoat, the weak evening sun making candlelight dance in her eyes.

'I better go for an ambulance then.'

She nodded. 'What about your coat?'

'Never mind about that,' he said, climbing the dune. Then he paused. 'I'm sorry about all this, I wish I could have done what he wanted.'

'It's better to be honest,' were her last words.

Then he was racing down the other side of the dune, and then through the others until finally he hit the strand, the long windy strand. The spindrift was flying inland like flock as he came upon his footprints and hers. Damn it, he hadn't even the courtesy to ask her her name. He was freezing without his coat. He stopped and looked about the blue and gold landscape.

'Honest she said,' he almost roared. 'I'm not honest, I can pretend the Gobi but I can't pretend to be a priest. But I pretend to be serene when I am the loneliest man in the whole world. Sweet Christ, I'm lonelier than Lonely Banna Strand.'

He crunched ahead. The Nat. Geog. would have to go. His mind was going technicolour and soft. He might as well yield to the shadows of the grey years that marched towards him like the dunes.

Away to the south, mountains purpled out of sight into the mists of Dingle. To the east the Stacks reared up saying thou shalt not pass. To the west was an endless sea, haughty in its wild commotion. To the north there would be something else, but he would not look back for was he not Tom Mullins, the man who stepped on his soul. He really didn't see anything, for now, the world was only as wide as a woman's face, or as narrow as the cold spot between the shoulder blades, and all he knew of Banna was the booming of the waves which would follow him all the way to the gates of the monastery. And thus the coldness grew within.

Prisoner of the Republic

All over Ireland marriages were going like slates off a roof but all the papers said that the law was finally catching up on its responsibilities, for today was the day after the Divorce Referendum and all would be settled. Bagnall wondered about this as he watched his colleagues yawn in the Remedial Law Section – mouths open, mouths shut – made them look like dogs barking in a silent movie. Somewhere there was a Law Reform Section but that was a silent movie also. So there was nothing to do anywhere except endure a Department of Justice life sentence, sit on your ass for forty years and hang your hat on a pension. They had all gone to law school and got law degrees, but being too feckless to rob the populace they had settled instead for the shabby security and awful certainty of the Civil Service. Now and again a law was brought in for resuscitation. This was done by upping the fine, redating it, turning colons into semicolons, and switching the small print around until the law shone like a new cup. So, thought Bagnall, we don't change the old laws and nobody makes new laws, could any nation ask for more.

Just now the law on weed control had been brought in and all over the office necks were trying to straighten out to cope with it. Fanaghan began to drone about the legal ramifications of ragwort, thistle and common dock, and how it was easily the most important law in the land. When one saw the fields of ragwort in Galway one understood why the country needed a Department of Justice. Fanaghan was very devout. Every Christmas he got post-coital depression which kept him out of work until St Patrick's Day. At lunch break he never went to the pub for a sandwich but remained behind to filch some kind of food from a brown paper bag. He didn't exactly eat it, he received it. His wife was very prominent in the

Clean Coin Society (Comann na mBonn nGlan) which was dedicated to the cause of erasing the balls off the bull on the fivepenny piece.

O'Lunasa rested his jaw on a pile of Irish dictionaries on his desk. He looked doleful as he explained his special problem. 'I have to translate every one of these damn laws into Irish, and in the case of ragwort there are at least twelve Irish words for it. The Irish have more words for a weed than the Eskimos for snow.'

Bagnall looked down at his law on dog control which was to prevent dogs crapping on the footpath. He pondered on this for a moment. Weeds and dog faeces! Suddenly it dawned on him for the first time what the Law was all about. It was to fight Nature and put it in its place. He grinned out at the sunshine on O'Connell Street and gave thanks to someone.

At that moment a trunkless head appeared at the door and announced that the law on horsedrawn traffic was three years overdue. Drinkwater who was working on it told everybody that he had it all under control, having just solved the problem of horseshoe nails. From now on all horseshoes would have six nails – this he discovered while on a junket to Bulgaria. O'Lunasa interjected and pointed out that seven would sound more euphonious in the Irish version of the law – a matter of eclipsis, he said. 'O.K., seven nails it is, so what the hell.' Ever since Drinkwater had reached the menopause he had been kicked down every Departmental stairs until he had finally lodged in Remedial Law, beyond which he could not go. But he was still ambitious and was angling for promotion to the Brehon Law section.

Thackerberry arose from behind his legal tomes and asked in a stutter, 'H-has anyone h-heard the latest report on the Referendum?' Nobody answered, for they all knew how Thackerberry had been thrown out of the house by his wife without even his bicycle clips, and how five years of litigation had reduced him to skin and bone. Bagnall surveyed the crumpled clothes and the tortured eyes. They said he was going out with someone new. Bagnall figured that any woman who was going to fall for Thackerberry was going to fall anyway.

'I h-heard that the first box from some island were all "yes" votes.' Heads down everywhere, nobody was going to get involved in a family argument. Thackerberry slowly made his way to the door and vanished – without even asking permission!

Mulfahy was office head and usually slept near the door with at least one eye open. He was addicted to Oriental takeaways which made him obese and, people said, also fluent in Chinese. Now he chortled and nodded a little, thus starting a chain reaction of lesser nods down a stairway of chins that vanished at his navel. It was a sign for everyone to spill out from behind desks laughing and talking at once.

'That island is Inishlavin, only one family on it.' Glee, glee. 'Possibly all Protestant.' Nasty political glee. Mulfahy doubled up, his bronchitic laughter sounding like swans flying in the distance. 'Thackerberry left his wife.' 'Then he's a bastard.' 'No his wife left him.' 'Then he's a hooroutahell.' 'It's going to be a landslide NO to divorce, anyway.' 'Who cares, price of a pint still the same.' 'Where did he get the name of Thackerberry anyway?' O'Lunasa's lip went xenophobic at the thought of going through life with the name of Thackerberry. Rooney said that separated people were all troublemakers and it was all sex anyway. 'The nearest I've come to sex in the last fortnight was squeezing a teabag,' said Connerty. O'Lunasa gave this some thought before he replied, 'the nearest I've come to sex was the genitive case.' Bagnall believed him for O'Lunasa was married to a redhaired haridan who raised spaniels by day and hell by night, a factor that caused him to delay in the office until hunted home by charladies. And still the weeds thickened.

Bagnall wondered why this circus didn't depress him as it usually did and then remembered that he had a magic charm against depression. 'Liz,' he said softly and then again, 'Liz.' Pure bloody magic. He smiled benignly at the human wreckage about him and felt full of sympathy for them all. And then he thought of what he was going to do to her after he met her at the Palace Bar and he got so randy he had to get up and move around. Anyway he believed that happy men should comfort the afflicted so he decided to follow Thackerberry. He winked at Mulfahy's eye and marched briskly out onto the street.

He found Thackerberry mooching around the street and joined him. He proposed that they both go to the nearest polling booth where the count was going on. Banners for both sides were up: Vote Yes, Vote No. 'Vote Yes' was a plea, 'Vote No' was a threat supported by Pope this and that, God, the Bible, and your chances of Kingdom Come. They strolled up to a woman manning a pro-divorce banner. She said it was bad, the votes from the countryside were killing them. And Ireland was all countryside. 'We need a miracle,' she said.

'Not going to happen,' said Bagnall mildly, 'why did you let the other side enlist God?'

'Well,' she said, 'He sort of is on their side.'

'God doesn't give a damn,' said Bagnall, 'why didn't you have a banner saying: "God doesn't give a damn, vote yes."?'

'Why didn't you tell us that a few days ago?' she retorted bitterly.

He turned away. She was right, only the passionate few took up the torch for any cause. Still, he felt it really was none of his business. Passing a woman who manned a NO banner he asked her what was happening. 'Justice is happening!' she said with Biblical disdain. They walked on in silence until Thackerberry stopped. His face tried to muster a wise expression but depression beat it off. 'Do you smell it?' he asked. 'What?' 'The air, it thickens with defeat, just like Kinsale, Aughrim and the Boyne.'

'Poetry! Come on I'll buy you a pint.'

They sat in silence over their pints.

'You going to be affected by this?'

Thackerberry thought for a moment and said, 'She's young, they don't hang about.'

'What about love?'

'What about it?' There was menace in the words.

'Well you know what Woody Allen said, "Better to have loved and lost," much better.' There was no reply. Bagnall listened to the millions of bubbles in their froth hissing and crushing, they sounded like the souls in purgatory shouting for water.

'How about you?'

'Oh, I'm O.K.,' said Bagnall, 'actually I'm in love.' He felt no embarrassment about saying it, for the first time ever. Not bad for a forty-year-old Irishman. He would have liked to tell him every-thing, like how they had met when she ran into his rear on the Naas dual carriageway. He had never claimed against her, but instead had taken the poor girl for a drink. After that it was plain sailing. Home to Mom and Dad in Tipperary by Lough Derg. Bagnall being a true Dubliner knew nothing about the countryside until taken in hand by her father and he learned what a hogget and a bushel was. Then the dew on the apples, the smell of cowdung, and the wind making waves in the barley. Fantastic! And country people! Time they tossed like a coin in the sun. He had drunk with her brothers and sifted through their unquestioning minds for stray lore on snipe traps, how to distinguish between the banshee and the neighbour's dog, why thunder turns milk sour and makes you forget your prayers, how not to get ringworm. Beautiful!

Back at the office the usual old thing, prop up the legal system by switching commas and colons. At 4.30 a head at the door announced total defeat for divorce. Thackerberry who didn't smoke asked for a cigarette. While he puffed at it eyes winked, lips curled, elbows longed to nudge. Then he headed for the door. On his way out Fanaghan asked him a little too pleasantly what he thought of the Referendum. 'Fuck them,' said Thackerberry. Fanaghan was taken aback and said rather smugly, 'I must say it doesn't interfere with my happiness.'

'Was your happiness put to a vote?' Thackerberry flung at him before he slammed the door. Mulfahy's eye jumped.

Bagnall also headed for the door.

Mulfahy stopped him. 'How's the law on cough bottles?'

'Sure I did that a month ago, I'm on dog control now.'

'Great stuff, have you come to the befouling the footpaths bit – I'm strong on that.'

'Befoul, befoul,' said O'Lunasa, as he dived for a dictionary.

'Christ deliver me,' whispered Bagnall as he made it to the street.

It was coming up to five o'clock and people were rolling into pubs like marbles. He breezed into the Palace Bar and ordered a hare and hound, an Irish followed by a pint of stout. He needed the wallop. He looked around, no sign of her yet. She was a calm girl, no fuss, never too early. Blake had said women were either mild silver or furious gold. She was mild silver and that was fine with him, although he would have liked sometimes a little fury for excitement. And he also expected that through the mild silver there was also the merest trace of iron. Like that day she had scared him, more than anybody ever. On a lovely day she had given Shep, the collie, her dinner and locked her in the stable, then taken Bagnall to the hayshed where six little balls of fur tumbled over each other to lick fingers and play with this new toy called the world. He picked them up delightedly, hugged them, kissed them. Then she took one and put him into a bucket of water. 'Stop, Christ, you'll drown it,' he had shouted. But she had said that's what had to be done, very simply, while bubbles and struggles tossed the water. Too many dogs – nobody wanted pups, that was it. He had pleaded with her. She said he didn't understand and all he could do was watch each pup play with the others to the last second till he was dunked. All gone. He had got sick on the straw. She had given him whiskey and taken him for a walk. But two things he would never forget, the sound of bubbles, and her expression as vacant as the sea breeze.

Suddenly he became aware of being watched in the mirror. She was there by the window all composed. 'Hi!' he said, going over to her with a big smile. He sat down, put his hand in his pocket, and carelessly threw a package on the table beside her. She looked down at the fancy paper.

'Jack – ' she said.

'Go on open it, it's for you.' She looked down at it again, her lips quivering, then she looked at him.

'Please put that in your pocket,' her intonation full of studied control. He did so.

'Later then, what'll you have to drink?'

'Jack it's all over.'

He looked at her, puzzled. 'What's all over, apple?'

She looked about her in desperation. 'It's all over between us and please don't call me apple, I hate it. You and me, finis.' She swallowed hard. 'Jesus, thank God I've said it, I've been going through agony.'

He stared at her in amazement. 'Me and you over? Why for God's sake?'

She clutched her handbag and tried to make herself smaller or shrink into her coat. 'Today, the Referendum, no divorce, we can't make it, we've had it.'

For a long time he stared at her, pale and lovely, though a little frightened, her knuckles white against her black bag. 'Liz, look, my marriage was only a joke, three months after, we split, she's in America now and happy. Eight years ago for God's sake, Liz.'

She closed her eyes, a bead of sweat appeared on her brow, her lips moved as if in prayer. 'My father, my brothers, they won't have it, there is money involved, theirs, mine. She's still your wife, she owns half of what you have now and the lot if you die, mine included, over my dead body. I'd have no rights. Huh! married to an F.U.I.!'

'An F.U.I.!' he whispered. It stood for 'fucked up Irishman/ woman', his own little way of describing the condition of being separated and Irish, now thrown at his face.

'I'm sorry, I don't want to hurt you, Jack, I didn't mean that.' Tears welled into her eyes only to be quickly brushed aside. She got up and stood against the window, still a little frightened, as if she expected him to assault her. He remained seated, trying to look cool. She bit her lip then tried to look cool, and succeeded. 'This isn't easy, Jack, I still love you, but not for e – not for, well, you know, time heals all.' Then as if he still didn't get her point she repeated quietly, 'Over, all over.' For a few seconds she stared at him in total calm then slowly turned away and walked through the door.

He remained sitting, trying to, trying to what? Understand? Yes, maybe understand, he supposed. It took people that had been hit by a car at least five minutes to figure out what hit them. But what was it that stuck in his mind about her? Yes, it was her expression, the same as when she drowned the pups. And why not? Had she not just drowned another. He tried to get up but only made it at the second try, and shuffled to the bar where his drinks still awaited him. He opened his mouth and fired them in willy nilly – no damn use – carbonic acid was the only drink from now on.

'Jesus, you look terrible, what's the matter?' It was Connerty who had sidled in beside him. Suddenly he had the urge to tell all, it would give immense relief. But then he remembered he was in Ireland, and for a man to bare his soul to another would be disaster, the merest hint of sorrow or defeat or trouble, especially in matters of the heart, would start a stampede for the door. He'd be shunned for years. 'My, my pup just drowned.'

'Ah, God, what a pity, how'd he drown?'

'Bucket of water.'

'Christ, man, how'd he do that?'

'A woman, she drowned him. He was the only pup I had.'

'A woman drowned him?' He turned to the others, 'A woman drowned this man's pup!' They gathered round. 'The hoors would do anything.' and 'Sue the bitch.' Well he was getting sympathy – but it was no use. Slowly they went back to their thoughts leaving Bagnall to peep at himself in the mirror.

Skerrit from Foreign Affairs sidled in beside him and dug into a pint. 'This country is a Banana Republic,' he said. Bagnall pointed out wearily that they didn't even have the climate for a Banana Republic.

'Get out, that's what I say,' said Skerrit.

'What do you mean?'

'Get out while you can, emigrate, get a wife, marry, happiness, what age are you?'

'Forty,' Bagnall said reluctantly.

'No good, forget it. No country wants forty-year-old genes, I know, I'm in Passports. South Africa maybe, police force, great future there.'

Jesus, deliver me, South Africa. Fat chance of a voice going down Fleet Street shouting 'new genes for old'. 'Looks as if all I've got is wisdom then.'

'There is neither a shilling nor an ounce of love in wisdom,' said Skerrit. He swigged his pint and wiped his mouth for inspiration. 'Wisdom is something I don't want,' he said, 'it is a little birdie telling you senility is just around the corner, it is a towel giftwrapped and thrown into the ring, it is an embalming fluid. Christ, give me the stupidity of youth any day.'

Suddenly Bagnall felt a terrible contempt for the land he had always loved. 'Do you know what' he said, 'I feel like going out and kicking in the telephone booths of this wretched country.'

'No, that would be vandalism. You could always go up and piss in the Garden of Remembrance.'

'What is it about the Garden of Remembrance that's worth remembering that I always keep forgetting?'

'Here comes Janie. Hi, Janie, over here,' said Skerrit.

Janie and Skerrit were both in the Remarriage Front; she came over, shocking news, Irish disgraced themselves again. 'Here, Janie, drink this, down the hatch.' They laughed and hugged and toasted each other, the cause, the fight, and they would always be righteous and noble. Bagnall was made aware of a new truth in life, that the sorest defeat is full of secret satisfactions. They were delighted they had lost; losers share more deeply than victors. And the camaraderie remained only as long as the cause. Had they won, their life's work of twenty years would have been laid waste. They would disband and drift to the grey suburbs where nothing stirs the heart.

He finished his drink because he couldn't take all this celebration of nothing beside him. He glanced around him: all the women in their twenties, where were the thirty-plus? Up in Rathmines washing their hair; washing and drying we lay waste our lives. Got to go, for he had a rule, only one disaster per pub. He took a last peek at himself in the mirror. He had read somewhere: 'If you look like your passport photo, you're too ill to travel.' He left in spite of this warning.

He found himself in a bar near Trinity staring at himself in the mirror. He looked as if someone had beaten him up. The feeling of loss is the worst because one's only reason for hanging on has abandoned one. It was as if a major part of his stomach was missing. He figured women felt like this after a miscarriage. A disaster had invaded his mind which was the same as putting a grand piano into an overfurnished room. Something had to be thrown out to make room. Humanity flees and whimpering self-pity holds the stage. In such melancholy he toasted himself in the mirror, praying for the easement of drink.

Boyle from the Department of Drains sat down beside him. 'I'm buying, forty quid I made in this Referendum. Sure anybody could see it didn't have a spud's chance in a sow's mouth. What'll you drink?'

'I'd rather drink my own blood.'

'That wouldn't be too good at the moment,' he said peering closely at Bagnall's face. 'You're like all the rest, don't understand this country. If you spent the first twenty years of your life on the edge of a bog you'd have enough insight into the Irish mind to last you a lifetime. Dublin is a slum for the unemployed, for the moment bog rules.'

It was time to drink his blood. 'I'll have that drink.' *Hoc est enim* corpus meum. Was Liz a bog man. No. But her father and brothers were. He had to blame someone. And her bloody awful friends Kate and Sinéad. Those two never concealed their dislike for him. He could imagine what it had been like the first day Liz told them about him. All down in the Arco kitchen, everything tasteful, the china, coffee and paté and crackers, the laughter, then the soft gossip, then the hard stuff, then – met Somebody New – civil servant – (nod, nod) – late thirties – sort of, well maybe, well looks young anyway – (approve, approve) – witty – (need that) pause, sip, sip, (more coffee?) – separated – (silence, swallow, swallow, two crackers crunch, belated emphatic nods, yes, lots of those cases, no problem, Sinéad ironing out invisible creases from skirt on ample thigh) – she loved him – (knowing nods, nothing like a bit of that, ... made all the difference) – and wasn't there a referendum coming, (yes, yes) – and would it win – (pause, pause, sip, sip, pick invisible fluff off cushions) of course, sure, weren't the Irish people a merciful lot, and who was for a whacker of brandy that Lenny brought home from Munich. And the shadows falling, falling, and deepening to fear within, and that little vein of iron flexing within the silver. The thought of her made him happy but then he remembered that she was gone and that blew him apart. He took one last look around him. Most Irish pubs looked like the inside of a whore's handbag. The cold air of the street kicked him in the chest and he grunted.

He landed in Morrissey's, Leeson Street, where a group of assorted Straights, Living Withs, Bigamists, Intacts, Celibates and F.U.I.s mingled and read the evening papers. Frawley bundled his and threw it into the basket. 'The provinces let us down. Screw Killarney's lakes and fells, I'm going down there no more.'

Land, a separated, turned from his paper. 'Talking about the news, did you hear how a Clareman knows when his pig is fat enough?'

'How?'

'When he farts he winks.' Everybody fell around. Somebody pointed at Land and said, 'He voted No.' Land polished his glasses and explained that one could have a much better time being the victim in a repressive society than a nobody in an enlightened one. Bagnall knew what he meant. Land was a predatory male and so charming he could whistle for women, whom he couldn't marry of course, so who'd want to change that. 'You fellas want to spoil the fun, the only defence a poor guy like me has against a pushy, grasping woman who wants to fall in love with you and carry you off to a cave, is repressive laws,' he said. Bagnall hated him but couldn't say anything, for he hadn't even voted. This did not stop him hating Land who had a mouthful of tongues all forked, and who was sly to the point of brain-damage. He was rich and believed like Rockefeller, 'them as has gits'.

Frawley stood Bagnall a drink and then began to drive him mad. He would suck in his breath, hold it, look sideways at nothing with the distant expression of someone pissing in the swimming pool, then exhale with a mighty swoosh, cough and say 'That's the way it is', or 'There you have it now.' Then he would address Bagnall with something like 'Love is like the world-food situation, those who love have so much left over they're throwing the stuff out while I have to live off the clippings of tin in Ethiopia'. Suddenly Bagnall wanted to be alone, he could no longer pretend an interest in desultory conversation, nor could he remain in the company of men who were at peace with themselves. 'Spanish ship in the harbour and not a whore in the house washed,' he muttered to himself, and then remembered that it was one of her father's sayings. He attacked his pint to leave. Frawley changed the subject to propose a kind of F.U.I. club, you know, meet, discuss the situation, policy, and of course socialise a bit, nudge, wink, you know have a few drinks while you're at it, you know sort of revolutionary. Bagnall thought about it for a minute. The thing about Ireland was that it had the climate for revolution but not the weather. Had the revolutionary Soviet met in Dublin instead of Moscow they would have drunk clockwise around Stephen's Green for ten years until Lenin would have bought a pub, Trotsky would have joined the Christian Brothers, and the only shot fired would have been by Stalin at a rat he kept seeing in his basement in Duke Street.

One last drink in Rathfarnham. The working-class pub with its T.V. blaring and the hard furnishings made it sound like Puck Fair on corrugated iron. It suited him for he would not meet anybody he knew. A whiskey helped to darken her face into memory, for memory is remembrance going stale, but not totally, for the voices of the lost speak to us for ever. A seller of Republican newspapers shoved *An Poblacht* into his face. All he could see was huge headlines proclaiming something about Republican prisoners. Bagnall shook his head. 'I'm not into that,' he said, and the man moved into the crowd. Still his befogged brain tried to grapple with some message he felt was in the phrase 'Republican prisoners'. Suddenly he knew what it was. He turned round to find the seller. He stopped him on the way out. 'It's not Republican prisoners we should be worried about,' he said, 'but prisoners of the Republic.'

'I don't get you,' said the seller.

'We're all prisoners of the Republic.'

'Who is?' he asked suspiciously.

'You, me, all of them, we are all prisoners of the Republic because of its repressive laws!'

The man looked oddly at Bagnall. 'I never heard o' them laws,' he said and left.

Bagnall decided he'd better go home or he would get drunk, so he staggered off to his car.

In his room on the Old Bawn Road, he paced in a kind of meandering way, as he tried to figure out what he was going to do with his life. Was he going to take up T.M., yoga, give up the drink, leave his job, go on macrobiotic food, learn Welsh, all of those idiotic things the defeated turn to for solace? Was he going to die here in a rage like a poisoned rat in a hole? One thing he knew for sure, he knew what had to be thrown out of his mind to make room for the Liz disaster: his love of Ireland. Give back to his country what she gave to him, contempt. He searched around for some symbol. That's when he saw his old hurley stick in the wardrobe; it was small and had followed him around from house to flat to room. He picked it up, felt its contours and its balance, then quickly snapped it in two on his knee. The sound it made was like the bark of a dog, but the feel was the feel of the small bones of someone he once knew in his childhood. He felt worse.

He walked to the window, pulled back the curtain and looked up. Stars jostled for a quick peep through holes in the sweeping clouds and all the while the great sky wheeling, wheeling. Soon dawn would peer through Ballinascorney Gap, bringing with it the first day of his life sentence as a prisoner of the Republic.

The Coffinmen

Once upon a time there lived the People, on a beach. Some were called Bananamen, who foraged deep in the jungle for bananas which they stored in secret places. The Viewmen occupied the most comfortable parts of the beach and congratulated each other on the view. The Doom-men visited everybody privately and whispered that the next wave might be their last. The Seermen stood in the water while they recounted the future and foretold the past. Finally came the Coffinmen. These quested deep in the Western Marsh, searching for the dying, comforting them in their last hours, and struggling vainly to save them. For saving the dead was the only thing that moved them to passion.

One day as a scout of the Coffinmen was searching the edge of the marsh, he heard a dinosaur boom out its unmistakeable goorawnk, goorawnk. Then he saw the ugly brute, its snakelike neck in clear relief against the setting sun. He was troubled. Later he asked another Coffinman if he had seen many dinosaurs lately.

'No, Brother, that I haven't.'

With great urgency the first man said, 'I think the dinosaurs are dying out.'

Quickly the death excitement of the Coffinmen came upon them. They looked at each other for a moment, the pallor of discovery on their faces, eyes locked in the common cause of death. And they raised a call – a super-call for a super-cause, and from far and near Coffinmen came crashing towards them. Hurriedly the council sat.

'What is your verdict?' asked the Chairman.

'The dinosaurs are dying out,' they said.

'Is there any hope?'

'There is no earthly hope.'

All sat tensely in the clearing, their eyes expectantly on the Chairman, as he mounted a mangrove stump.

'Fellow Coffinmen, the dinosaurs are dying out. Let there be no doubt about that. They are lost – I repeat lost.' Then with fervour, the Chairman spread his hands to the skies, and intoned, 'All those in favour of saving the dinosaurs say Aye.'

'Aye!' roared the assembly with such violence that all the pterodactyls burst from their trees in fright. The Coffinmen hugged each other in delighted triumph, the triumph of a lost but common cause, and they marched off into the jungle singing their anthem. In the distance an agonised goorawnk was heard as the noble cause sank deeper into the mire.

Next day the Coffinmen set about saving the monsters, as they plunged, floundered or sank into the swamp. They noticed for the first time their elegant necks, their graceful lumbering, their noble struggling, and these observations urged the Coffinmen to feats of energy as they tied vines to the creatures and heaved them on to firmer ground. Righteous sweat rolled down their cheeks as they dragged the monsters all over the marsh. Then long lines of Coffinmen crisscrossed the place as they passed bananas to the famished beasts. They smacked their chops and goorawnked in gratitude. But some had sunk too far. On these was lavished love. Tender bamboo shoots, the soft tops of ebony trees, and sweet mahogany bark – the choicest titbits of the jungle – were fed to them. Until they vanished leaving tell-tale bubbles to mark the transience of noble agony.

Then it was noticed that the monsters began to lose all reason. They flopped about uncaringly and when they sank dangerously they just calmly waited for the Coffinmen to heave them out. Then the Bananamen came and complained that all the bananas were being given away to bloody serpents.

'Traitors!' roared the Coffinmen with such vehemence that all the ripe bananas dropped in clusters to the ground. The Bananamen departed for good.

But the monsoon came and the Coffinmen fled in disorder to the beach. After the rains they hared back to the marsh. Nothing to be seen – save for the odd coelecanth that splashed in the waterholes. All day they searched and towards evening a snout was discovered half an inch above the muck. It took three days to dig him out. He emerged, bemused but grateful. They gathered round him and stroked his muddied flanks. Each Coffinman wanted to help and each brought gifts of food. The old monster ate them. The jungle all round was being defoliated but he just ate and ate, eyes and cheeks bulging. Even when his jaws sagged the Coffinmen gave him no rest, but plied him with dainties. One day after a treeful of mangrove fruit he burst apart with a sorrowful goorawnk.

There was shock; all gathered round; they coaxed, they tickled, they prodded. No good.

'The dinosaurs are dead,' somebody said, and the Coffinmen hung their heads. A sob was heard, tears fell, someone tore out his hair. But the Chairman roared, 'Let us bury the mighty, the fallen, with dignity. On with the Cause.'

They dug a big hole and the last of the dinosaurs was laid to rest. Speeches were made. The Chairman stood on a mangrove root and shook his fist at the skies and shouted with passion. 'The Beauty of the world doth make us sad – this Beauty that will pass, but the fools, the fools, they have left us our Dinosaur Dead, and in Death shall they repose with us till time and time is done. Long live the Dinosaurs.'

Suddenly a call was heard in the distance. It was the secret death-call of the Coffinmen. All watched the scout as he dashed across the marsh.

'The dodo,' he spluttered, 'the dodo is dying out.'

'Are you sure?' asked the Chairman.

'No doubt about it,' said the scout, 'they all have their beaks stuck in the ground and they won't budge.'

'That's bad,' everyone said.

'Silence!' roared the Chairman. 'All those in favour of saving the dodo, say aye!'

'Aye!' roared the Coffinmen with such fury that all dying things in the vicinity died a little more. And they marched off in triumph singing their death anthem.

But a few remained, bemused, forlorn. They shambled round the grave looking out over the great marsh. Slowly one of them climbed on to a rock and said to the others evenly, 'Who said the dinosaurs were dead?' Nobody answered.

There was a holy smile on his face and the sun glinted in his passionate eyes.

'Goorawnk,' he said.

'Goorawnk, goorawnk, goorawnk,' they all replied, and they danced around the grave, clapping their hands and nodding in secret communion, as they did, they waved their necks in stark relief against the setting sun.

The Isle of Geese

Somewhere behind the mill shone the sun and that's why the kitchen was in gloom. Somewhere in the town his mother scrubbed doorsteps and that's why he sat smoking instead of doing things. Somewhere a war was over and people said 'twas just as well. He could keep on saying somewhere this and somewhere that and it would never come to an end. That wouldn't do because he had responsibilities.

Out in the street he listened to the sweet trot of donkeys in harness, or the heavy honest bootfall of a countryman in town. He had to stop pretending that these sounds were important and should be investigated; because – today was the day.

He sat in his father's huge armchair and tensed his muscles; somehow the strong oak made him feel more solid. But his father had not been allowed to finish it, so sitting in it also made him feel a little incomplete. Especially of late, something was lacking. It was some strange hunger that comics, swims or sweets would not satisfy. Nor was it easy to disguise it as just another complication in his thirteen and a half years of life.

'Rex!' he commanded. A white wire-haired terrier appeared at his master's feet, its erect tail docked to the level of its alert head. He patted its neck, but took care to avoid the red flame that spread along its back. A kennelsman had come to look at it. 'Get rid of him,' he said. 'Is there no hope, sir?' 'None,' and he had gone with disgust on his face.

He thought of saying a few words, but he felt that only the condemned had the right to speak. He stood up and topped his Woodbine, fitting it carefully into a secret hole in his jacket. He opened the window a little to clear the air, not from fear of reprisal but out of respect. They had an understanding; widows and only sons always do.

He had no lead for the dog, so after some rummaging he found a red bathrobe girdle; they had no bath in the house. The dog whined as he felt his neck encircled, and suddenly tried to bolt for the yard but the silk girdle held.

'Come on now, Rex, come for a walk.' He clicked his tongue, but it was no use; he dragged him across the floor, the dog's nails scraping in vain for purchase on the worn tiles, his jaws locked on the girdle, poison in his terrier's eyes. Colm clenched his teeth and tugged him out onto the street, dragging him on his behind down through the gutter. The dog tumbled, snarled, frothed and tried to wrap himself round things that weren't there, but he was tiring. Colm glanced over his shoulder, fearful that anybody should see this pitiful relationship between dog and master, fearful he should be thought cruel. His mother had promised rashers for tea, and eggs maybe; it wasn't enough.

Quickly he dodged up the alleyway at the mill, hurrying the dog along with scoldings and little promises, leaving an inquisitive street behind. At the end of the alley they emerged onto the Isle of Geese, a network of ruins, now rose-red in the evening sun. It was the town's riddle: where was the isle, where were the geese? Some said it was cursed, but couldn't remember why or by whom. Others said that once the gentry had lived there, then tenants, then squatters, but even they had moved out. The chimneys were built with craft and love, for only they now stood upright, the walls had long since spilt their loads in the sun. Now nobody knew who owned the place and nobody cared, for it was good for nothing except loving by night and slaughtering by day.

Suddenly Rex gave up the fight and trotted out in front of him. They dodged the pools of animal urine which soaked up the last of the evening's rays. He stopped outside the slaughterhouse. It was a ruin that managed a roof and gave some protection to the rows of carcases that hung from the rafters. A familiar sight, it never failed to awe him. He looked through the tiny barred window at their red and white flanks glowing in the gloom. Somehow they embarrassed him; they were naked and ought to be covered, he thought. In the middle of the floor stood the slaughter-post, its well-polished steel

ring like an evil eye in the half light. Colm padded across the straw
and looped the girdle through it. Somewhere out in the backyard he
could hear the faint song of the whetstone tampering with the
silence; skilled hands were honing something, maybe an axe. The
dog whined. The song made the boy uneasy, but it also excited him,
for this was the only place in the town where anything interesting
happened. He and his companions had often spent hours gaping
when there would be a big kill – a dozen sheep, four bullocks, a pig
or two. He would never forget the day that the bullock broke loose,
snapping the rope when he smelt the blood and smashing his way
through the half door, eyes outraged. For half an hour he had run
amok in the Isle, bellowing with terror and scattering bricks and
mortar. But the men trapped him and stout hands and chains had
dragged him back to the slaughter-post for there was no reprieve
from the Isle of Geese.

He walked to the back door and looked out on the yard. Over in
the corner lay the offal heap: a colourful medley of hearts, bellies,
livers, entrails, sheep's heads and assorted tails. His stomach
couldn't stand it, so he turned back to the slaughter and sidestepped the carcasses over to the tool-rack. There neatly arranged
was a complete set of butcher's knives, cleavers and axes, all curved
and gleaming in the weak light. Reverently he removed the biggest
and deadliest from the rack. He clasped the black handle in his small
hand and tested the edge; it was like a razor. Suddenly he lurched
forward and ran the air through and through, then unexpectedly
swivelled and slashed viciously at his rear, his mouth twisted with
aggression. He looked down at the glistening blade; he longed for
something to test it on, a branch of a tree, or a bed of tall ferns.

The dog whined meekly, and his ears stood; he looked over with
soft brown eyes that couldn't gauge their master's mood and craved
some sign. Colm clicked his tongue and Rex wagged a half-
reassured tail.

Steel-heeled boots thumped across the cobbled yard, and Jimmy
Colgan's frame darkened the whole slaughterhouse as he came in
the back door. 'Put that away or you'll cut the hand off yourself,' he
said, as he crossed to the rack leaving carcasses swinging in his
wake. He hung two axes and a cleaver on the rack. 'Big kill tomorrow, boy, six bastes – bit fat ones – enough to feed the army.' Colm

looked up at the powerful hairy arms; they had blood on them, and blood on the leather apron. He looked at the fat red face – it shone with condition; steak three times a day, the people said.

'Well I suppose you want something?'

'Maybe you'd kill the dog for us.'

'Why can't ye kill him yeerselves? I'm a busy man,' said he, heaving sheeps' fleeces onto a pile.

'Well, I said to drown him in the Basin, but Ma started crying.'

'Go on now,' said the butcher, who began to survey the carcasses.

'Oh, yes she did,' he continued eagerly. 'Da gave me Rex as a present before I was born. Did you know he is four and a half months older than me?'

'I did not. Hand me over that chopper.'

'And then I said I'd lose him up the Glen, but she wouldn't hear of it.'

'Of course she wouldn't. She said, "Go down to Jimmy, he has nothing else to do."'

'No, no, she did not, she left it completely up to myself,' and he smiled proudly. 'Maybe you would use the gun on him.' The butcher dropped the chopper on the table. 'Where the hell does the town think I get bullets from, down with the showers of rain, is it?'

The boy winced; he had been told that too much meat made a man cranky. He looked away out through a hole in the wall. 'Ma said that you and Da were "out" in the Troubles together.'

The butcher looked down at the bloodstained straw and thought hard as if it was something he hadn't remembered in years. He glanced at the boy and at the dog tied to the slaughter-post. His voice had an unusual mildness. 'Yes we were, and what's our thanks? Tadhg is dead and I'm a shooter of dogs. It's been a long time all these years. I'm down to a few bullets, but there's one for you, Moriarty,' and he set about removing the Colgan's dinner from a ram's carcass.

Colm was encouraged. 'Was Da big, really?' he asked.

Jimmy was surprised. 'Tadhg was a giant, a walking giant.'

'Yes, but was he strong though?' he asked urgently.

'Strong, is it you said?' and he looked around for something heavy. He wrapped his arms around a hanging bullock, his cheek pressed into the flank, and he strained. His face was red with exertion as he gasped – 'Your father would lift that baste, no bother to him.'

Colm was exultant; it was better, he thought, to have a powerful dead father than a weak live one. He had examined the surviving fathers of the town; they were a sorry lot.

Jimmy walked over and glanced down at the dog. 'I'll do the job now in a jiffy. Tell me, is he much good as a ratter?'

'Not at the moment I'd say. I hear you have trouble with the rats.'

'Trouble is it, they're taking over the Isle of Geese, the black, sinful scourge.' He strode out to the yard and pointed at the offal heap in triumph. 'Look!' A long sheep's gut was being tugged down a rat-hole at the base of the wall. Jimmy picked up a ram's head and flung it with all his might; it struck the red brick like a drumbeat. The gut stopped for a moment, but the tugging picked up almost immediately. 'There you are, you can't beat them.' He looked down at the ground, eyes penetrating deep below the bloodied cobbles. 'There must be millions down there,' – his steel heel tapping out their location to Colm. 'Jaysus, there's nothing I want more than a good ratter, a knacky terrier, a hungry wan. Trap 'em, poison 'em, smoke 'em out, burn 'em, drown 'em, they still come back.' He looked in at the hanging carcasses. 'Thanks be to Christ the hoors haven't got wings or this town could starve.' He stood in the middle of the yard, chopper at the ready as if he expected he'd have to make a stand any moment against the black peril. 'I read in a book, once, a terrible thing,' he was almost whispering. 'It said that rats were so clever that they could rule the world like man.'

'And why don't they so?' said Colm.

The butcher was taken aback; puzzled eyes searched the cobbles. 'The book didn't say; I suppose Our Lord stopped them,' he said simply.

They left the yard and walked back to the tool-rack, neither of them glancing at the dog which sat on the ground, his tail worrying the straw, eyes begging some small acknowledgement. A little whine failed to dislodge his master; this was no ordinary evening.

Jimmy picked up an axe and passed it to Colm. 'Hold that against the stone for me.' He himself sat on the stool and worked the treadle with his feet, making the great whet-stone spin rapidly. 'Hold it down more or you'll destroy the edge on me, down more, that's it.'

Sparks circled up from the silvering blade, there was a dull song in the air, and Colm felt great comfort in the smooth curve of the axe-handle. They had no axe at home; and he was proud to be trusted with such a deadly weapon.

'That's why I hate rats, they're there but you can't see them.'

'I often saw one.'

'You did, but did you see the hundreds of others that were watching you?'

'No I suppose.'

'There you are, just like I said, they're there but you don't see them.' He took the axe over to the light of the small window and eyed the gleaming crescent; he was satisfied. 'You know,' he said in admiration, 'edge is one of the most important things in life, it makes for swiftness and cuts out butchery.'

He hung the axe and took down a bundle of oily rags from the cubby-hole. He peeled off the rags and grasped a blue-black revolver. The boy gasped when he saw it and moved up closer. Round barrel, rectangular handle, curved trigger. Jimmy broke it, cocked it, triggered it and spun it with ease. To Colm the sounds were cold, efficient and deadly.

'Do that again, Jimmy, please,' he said excitedly. Jimmy smiled with satisfaction; the gun snapped and spun in his hand once more. Suddenly the movements stopped and Colm found himself staring down an unwavering barrel pointed between his eyes. He tried to look down the spout of the gun, but it was dark in the barrel; it was like looking down a rat-hole. He found himself quaking inside.

'Take your dog out to the gable of the slaughter, Moriarty.'

'Why out there?'

'Because there's earth enough to bury him – earth, boy.'

He fumbled with the silken lead, but the dog almost dragged him out of the house. They waited until Jimmy appeared.

'Sit,' the boy said with authority, clicking his fingers at the same time; slowly the dog sank back on its haunches, never taking his eyes off his master.

'Do you think he'll stay sitting down?'

'Yes,' he answered with pride and certainty in his voice, 'he's very well trained.'

Jimmy went on one knee beside him. 'By God, that's a pity

because in two minutes he's going to be the best-trained, deadest dog in the Isle of Geese.

The safety catch clicked. He peered closely at the dog.

'That's funny,' he said.

'What?'

'His nose, it's as damp and shiny as as blackberry.'

'What about it?'

'That's the sign of health in a dog, you know. Seeing the state he's in, I'd say it should be dry.' As if to convince himself he tested it with his finger. A pink tongue curled round it, licking it and the other fingers, then extending to the blood-stained palm and wrist. The hand was not withdrawn. 'There's a nice dog, oh yes, a great little fellow altogether.' Jimmy crooned with pleasure. 'And nice eyes in a fine head too, he's no mongrel anyway. 'Tis a shame he can't be cured.'

''Tis.'

Jimmy patted the dog's head and stood up. 'You'll have to shoot your own dog, Moriarty.'

Colm looked up sharply at the butcher. 'What do you mean?'

'Just what I said, you're going to have to shoot this dog yourself.' The boy was completely taken aback. He looked up at the man's red face and then down at the dog who hadn't taken his eyes off him once. 'I couldn't do it,' he said nervously, 'anyway you're the butcher.'

Jimmy closed one eye and squinted shrewdly at the rubble of the Isle of Geese. He spoke like a man who decided to give away the secret of his profession. 'Yes, I'm a butcher, I'd kill any class of an animal they brought into the Isle of Geese, on wan condition mind you, that I don't look into their eyes, for all eyes are sort of human.'

They both looked down at the brown eyes that begged some slight token of recognition.

'I'd miss; I'd be no good with a gun,' he said tensely.

'You couldn't miss with this.' He snapped the gun shut and sighted along the barrel at old rusty wash-tubs, chimney-pots and distant steeples. 'Can't miss, come on, you've the day destroyed on me.'

The sun sank behind the tallest chimney, its long shadow slicing the Isle of Geese in two. The safety catch clicked back on and the gun was pushed into Colm's hand. It was hard and cold and he never expected it to be so heavy; he didn't dare look down; it made his stomach feel empty and also hungry with excitement. His grasp tightened on the butt and his finger felt along the curving trigger-guard. There was great power in a gun, he felt; he could stand up at the back of the class and plaster Brother Barry to the blackboard. He could terrorise the town. He could swagger down Castle Street, jaw set, eyes dead ahead and calmly watch huxters, farmers and fishwomen scamper down side-streets out of his way.

'Will you hurry up?'

Colm's voice quivered: 'Can I practise on something first, please, Jimmy?'

'No, you cannot. I've no bullets.'

'Well, can I just aim at things so?'

'Alright, but hurry up or I'll take it away from you.'

Slowly he raised the heavy blue-black weight; it looked so out of place in his pink hand. He was pointing at one of the few remaining walls in the Isle. His gunner's eye squinted down the barrel, picking out the sight through the V. It was dead centre of the wall. He felt all the power of his mind and soul surge down his arms, down the spout of the gun. He could blast a hole big as a doorway in that wall, scattering stones and mortar. His hand was steady now.

'Shoot,' the voice whipped the air.

The boy swivelled, the butcher watched, the dog sat. There was a blast, a blotch of red, a threshing of white. The ruins fragmented the blast into a thousand echoes which spread out across the Isle, scouring deep into rat-holes. From every chimney, showers of nesting starlings exploded into the air, making the place thick with wings. He had never expected the gun to buck in his hand, never realised it was such a live and powerful thing. Nor did he feel the strong fingers which prised the gun out of his hand. He felt very little except the emptiness of words such as – kill, gun, dead, shoot. The prone figure bewildered him, it was so white, so red, so still. The whirring in the air was dying now, for the chimneys were sucking the starlings back again as if they had only loaned them. He leaned forward and his dry throat croaked: 'Rex.' This time more of a statement.

'Your dog is dead, you shot him,' quipped Jimmy as he passed him. 'There's a spade for you, start digging.'

Colm hardly heard him; he sat on his hunkers beside his dog, his face ashen, his fists tightly clenched against the revulsion he felt rising within himself.

'I didn't want to shoot my dog,' he said, almost choking.

Jimmy's foot drove the spade into the crisp earth.

'He's not your dog any more. You can't own the dead, sonny.'

"Twas you made me do it,' he replied in anguish.

'Come on, you're a big boy now, what else would you have done with him?'

'I could be walking now out the bank with him.'

'And the state he was in?'

'I wouldn't mind.' Tears welled down the boy's face.

'Your mother wouldn't put up with him.'

'She would, I know.'

Jimmy, who was clearly exasperated, opened his arms and appealed to the Isle of Geese: 'And what in Christ's name did you shoot him for so?'

'Cause she left it up to me,' he moaned, tears and sobs following freely; nor did it seem to matter to him that his tears were being observed. Jimmy stood for a moment, the revolver dangling from his finger, his gaze falling carelessly on the ruins before he turned and walked back slowly to the slaughterhouse. The boy took Jimmy's going as a hint, grasped the spade and began to dig; he unearthed bits of clay-pipes, teapots, old bottles – all the trappings of forgotten comfort. It was hard to dig and it made him puff, each breathful of air laden with cordite searing his lungs. He heard the voice inside the slaughterhouse, 'I'll get ye both a pup, a nice shepherd pup for nothing. Tell your mother that.' The boy continued to dig, or scrape rather, for he felt it was like digging through a kitchen floor. He didn't care and he barely leaned on his spade. After a while words were shouted out through a hole in the slaughterhouse wall, 'Bury him deep, boy, deep, think of the rats,' and a steel heel tapped the cobbles. He tasted his own tears and swallowed. He was disgusted; he could feel the dark evil things watching him. With a new energy he attacked the ground, but his small grasp couldn't manage the spade handle.

Jimmy stomped out of the slaughterhouse, removed the spade

from him and began to shovel, excavating bricks and earth in showers; it was as if each spadeful was a blow against rats. The boy forgot his sorrow long enough to feel and admire the might of this grave-digger who could do violence to any part of the Isle. The dog's white form was laid snug in the hole and covered forever beneath a ceremony of tiles and other cracked and useless things. Jimmy hammered them all into a gentle mound. He leaned gasping on the spade, grey wisps stuck with sweat to his forehead.

'Go home now, Moriarty, 'tis almost night. Tell the town I'm shooting no more dogs, the day of the slaughterhouse is done. Abattoir is the new word; we'll all be leaving the Isle of Geese.'

Colm moved quickly away in silence; he wondered what the man meant by 'all', for there was only himself. The chimneys' shadows were now stretched to their limits, probing among the rubble. Soon the place would be engulfed in one great shadow. He shivered.

'Hey! Hey!'

He looked back at Jimmy who was still standing by the grave; he held the red girdle in the air. 'I've a use for this if you don't want it,' he shouted.

'You're welcome to it.' Colm hurried down the lane that led from the Isle and he emerged on to the street. A cart dashed by, a drunken farmer singing and beating the horse pitilessly. It was a familiar sight which reassured him in his loneliness, in his feeling of having done a great wrong. He paused in the mouth of the laneway before deciding that he wouldn't go home yet. He didn't want rashers, he didn't want meat. He wanted to be alone; there was no better place than the main street of the town.

The Doomsday Club

It was so quiet in the Doomsday Club that you could hear the spiders spin their webs in the dry corners of their universe. Quiet because hope had been banished, and hope brings noise, and only in despair is there unqualified peace. We had investigated the outside world only to discover that hope also caused wars whereas despair ended them. The world was upside down – virtue was the enemy of man.

And so we enshrined in the club constitution the qualifications for membership. Only people of a despairing, melancholy and negative disposition could become members. Those who were dedicated to desperation were barred, for any kind of dedication in a world that was doomed was a contradiction.

However, an analysis of the early membership showed a disturbing trend. The club was filling up with Irish speakers. It appeared that in matters of pure negation they had no equal. With them as a bonus came other admirable human qualities such as spite, jealousy, envy, sloth, pride, bitchery and begrudgery. To fall in line with the Futility Clause which is the cornerstone of our constitution, we agreed to join them and speak only the Irish language which is so doomed that each morning we have to check that it is still there. Soon we were all convinced that the Celtic way of doom was more poetic.

Nobody was in charge of the Doomsday Club, for that would be an overture of neatness, a recognition that order had a place in our dying world. Futility and despair were things of beauty that gave the necessary cohesion to our group. It would also be suicidal for anyone to contemplate leadership for we would batten on his strength like leeches, we would hate him into sickness, hurt him into shame, hound him to an early death. Woe to the head that would raise itself above the crowd. For sustenance we had our dream, the dream of Celtic supremacy over the nations of the earth. We had examined the dreams of others and decided that ours was the safest, for never would our dream be touched by the sordidness of this world.

None of us were native speakers of Irish but once we did have one as a member. He continually bewailed our poor grasp of cliché and corrected our grammar. We expelled him under the Perfection Clause. And so we practised our bad Irish, drank beer and generally sat around, waiting for the trumpet blast that would tear the skies apart, doom us all and get it over with.

Only one woman, Iníon Ní Chuísosaigh, succeeded in getting in, mainly because she was in Women's Lib. and that fitted in nicely with the Futility Programme. She always came late, drank vodka and when she spoke, which was rarely, insisted on using the Imperfect Subjunctive. She always had the grace to leave before closing time. (Closing time came when the last member fell dead drunk on the floor.)

The first indication we had of the Second Coming was in the strange behaviour of one of our members. Críostóir Ó Maoil Íosa was a man who drank pints faster than Irish was dying, which left him continuously intoxicated. However, he began to develop Christ-like qualities such as beating us all to the round of drinks. Kindness was against the rules but the way we looked at it that was his problem.

He also took to wearing a beard and developing those eyes that followed you around the room like those of the picture of the Sacred Heart. When he finally appeared in a flowing white robe we knew that something was afoot. Finally he simply indicated to us all that he would like to apply for planning permission for one crucifixion. We were not allowed by the rules to show our delight. Delight is only allowed at the funerals of colleagues. On being asked his reasons he explained that he didn't think his name in Irish, Christopher the Follower of Jesus, was a coincidence. We knew there was no such thing. And he was also an Irish speaker. Why should God choose an Irish speaker for the Second Coming, we asked. He replied that God had a hangup about linguistic scenarios, having chosen the Aramaic Gaeltacht for his First Coming. (The beauty

about the Doomsday Club is that one doesn't have to be logical.)
The Irish language was moribund and its speakers degenerate, it
had eighteen different words for telescope, it had resisted many
attempts to standardise it while each new dictionary confounded all
that went before. Its speakers were so devious that they had devised
no exact word for 'yes' or 'no'. The result was a permanent commit-
ment to uncertainty. And there was no word for 'have' in the
language. The 'have', 'yes', and 'no' problem gave rise to the
ridiculous situation where one could not translate the words of the
immortal song 'Yes, we have no bananas'. Was it any wonder he
said that he had taken up the study of Manx, Cornish, and Old Irish,
three languages that were safely dead.

We commended his bitchery but pointed out that we were still not
happy with his answer. Desperation leaked out of his eyes and
pulled and tugged at the muscles of his face (he had the kind of face
that one would dearly love to crucify). He finally gasped that if man
were created in God's likeness then there was a possibility that God
had a sense of humour. This was satisfactory but then we came to
the tricky bit: we informed him that in the matter of sacrifice,
especially self-sacrifice, a benefit usually accrued to the survivors
and that the bestowal of benefits was contrary to the spirit of the
constitution. He said he was disappointed in us and that his only
motivation was the sheer and utter waste of it all. We were so
pleased that we immediately granted him full planning permission
for one crucifixion. We appointed a crucifixion committee to assist
him in his undertaking and wished him every success. The agreed
day was the following Good Friday. As an afterthought we asked
him if he believed in God. He drew himself up to his full height and
replied with dignity, 'I am God', we were quite pleased, an Irish
speaking God and high time too. We celebrated by getting him to
buy us all a round of drinks.

At the first meeting of the crucifixion committee Críostóir, who
will henceforth be called the Subject, stood on the stage, slowly
releasing the aura of martyr, evangelical light, a good hundred
watts, radiating from his eyes. He requested that the writer, de
Brún, be allowed to script the whole affair but cautioned him to
avoid the sentimentality of the original. Mac Cartagáin, who was an
engineer, was elected stage manager. The latter, being a person of

some dynamism, proceeded immediately to measure the Subject's vital statistics in order to get the dimensions of the cross right. There was spontaneous applause and many offers of hammers and nails. But the Subject indicated that even though his life up to this had been a stunning failure (failure was obligatory for us all), he felt that one request for uniqueness should be granted to him: namely to have the distinction of being the only person ever crucified on a Celtic cross. The hammers-and-nails set were disappointed with this news because Celtic crosses are made of stone. They argued with him, pointing out that Celtic crosses are small and he might find them too confining. But the Subject said confinement had been the Celtic lot and to go in such a manner would be more poetic.

After a while Mac Cartagáin said he knew where he could get a cement cross. The Subject thanked him and asked him if he could make it three because he felt he might like a little support. This was going to be great, three crucifixions, we had forgotten the thieves. Somebody pointed out that we didn't have any thieves in the club. Mac Cartagáin said that he could hire a couple of Irish-speaking actors – not only unemployed, but also out of work. There wasn't much point in crucifying them because already the disposal of bodies was a problem high on his list. At the mention of bodies the evangelical light wavered a little in the Subject's eyes.

How, someone asked, was the Subject to be nailed to a cement cross? That was no problem said the stage manager. He then explained to us the workings of the Hilti gun nail-driver, which with the aid of an explosive cartridge could drive a steel bolt into the cement. The Subject would not feel a thing, he felt. The Subject looked quite concerned. Somebody mentioned that it would be one hell of a job getting the Subject off the cross, what with the Hilti nails and all. But Mac Cartagáin said that was a bridge we would cross in good time. Críostóir began to look a little forlorn at this stage and he asked what preparations had been made for his scourging at the pillar. The script writer came forward and said he had written it out of the script. He didn't mind a little crucifixion, but he was totally against blood sports. Still and all, the Subject said, he felt entitled to some ceremony. As an overture to this we offered Iníon Ní Chuíosaigh the part of Veronica *i.e.* to wipe the face of the Subject. Her answer was unprintable, which we took as a refusal. At this point the Subject began to complain and said, granted we couldn't have too much ceremony but there should be some flourish, something exotic, romantic even, something eloquent of the Celtic story. We told him that the Celtic story was the most tawdry record in the annals of *Homo Sapiens*, that from the Celtic Dawn to the Celtic Twilight was such a sordid picture of treachery, slyness and rascality, that the Celts deserved to become extinct – and that only in the official Club Celtic Dream was there preserved some modicum of dignity. Celts lived in misery during the day, went to bed at night with defeat and only in the morning did the prospect of failure give them the will to persevere.

A Cambell from the Isles offered to play the bagpipes during the highlights of the occasion. The Subject thought about it and said he'd like a lament. We offered him a choice of 350 laments for the 350 battles we had lost and five laments for the one we won. We finally settled on 'Phil the Fluter's Ball', much to the annoyance of the Subject. The stage manager said that talk about battles had reminded him that we needed a spear. Somebody said he could steal one from the railings of an old Protestant Church. We weren't mad about the idea because we wanted to keep religion out of it. There was much discussion among the technically minded about how best to sharpen this spear for the purpose in hand. It was at this time that we noticed that the Subject's evangelical light had dwindled to a leak from his left eye, and within his white robe his proud bearing had begun to droop somewhat. He was asked if he wanted to go through with the being offered vinegar on a sponge bit. Somebody suggested that it should be stout seeing as it would be his last taste ever. This latter helpful remark and the stage manager's secret plan (no point in bothering the Subject) for the disposal of the body, which involved a J.C.B., combined to give Críostóir Ó Maoil Íosa's face a look of deep disappointment – unreasonably we thought in the circumstances. The proceedings were concluded.

On Good Friday the Standing Committee for Linguistic Co-ordination was in full swing in the club. We were endeavouring to translate 'Yes, we have no bananas' into terms that would be in keeping with the genius of the language. We decided to take the bull by the horns and hijack the verb *habeo* from the Latin which means *I have*, thus bestowing on the Irish Language a new concept of ownership. It went like this: *Habaim, Habann Tú, Habann Sé, etcetra.* We agreed that *Habann tú banana?* sounded bad enough but *sea, ní habaimid aon bhannanaí* was so dreadful that it should be adopted as standard straightaway. We hadn't time to put it to a vote because just then a young woman burst into the room demanding her money immediately. It transpired she was referring to the crucifixion of our former member, now deceased, at which she attended as a Mary Magdalene, she already being a whore from Fitzwilliam Square. She spoke no Irish but as she was black and spoke English so badly we deemed her negative enough to deserve a hearing (the Irish are so virtuous they have to import whores).

She said crucifixions were a waste of men, that she wanted her money and that she was waiting for no 'resurrection'. There was immediate consternation – there was no planning permission for a resurrection. She made matters worse by saying that the ruffians had taken great delight in the business. Groups such as ours always had their enemies within, and our constitution always lived under the threat of positivism. In our case the Optimism Lobby and the Happiness Faction waited their chance to seize authority. We decided to investigate so we put the whore out.

De Brún, the script writer said it was a terrible crucifixion with everyone departing from the script, especially the Subject. When the latter had announced that he intended to resurrect, the script writer had given him a warning. But he insisted, saying that he intended to do it the following Tuesday. Everybody pleaded with him to resurrect on a bank holiday or on a weekend but not on a Tuesday which was a workday. But he had been adamant. He said he was in bad shape and, try as he might, he knew he wouldn't make it till Tuesday. Everyone was so annoyed that they proceeded to dispatch him immediately. His last words were that when he arose he would make an important announcement for all humanity which he wanted published in all the local papers.

This resurrection thing was a bad business. A live member we had some control over but a deceased member could say anything, for we had lots of secrets – real compromising stuff. Then we discussed the event of his resurrection and asked for suggestions as to the possibility of his rehabilitation within the club. Everybody was against it, saying he'd be cut up pretty bad and an embarrassment to us all. Furthermore the Achievement Clause ruled out his being taken back. Mac Cartagáin said it was ridiculous to seriously consider his resurrection because he had with his J.C.B. dug a large hole in the hill and rolled a massive granite boulder over it. He'd never move that stone, he said. Still, just in case, we decided to attend the affair on Tuesday.

All day on Tuesday we waited on the little hill, watching the mountain fog swirl about the lonely crosses – and of course the stone – we really watched that stone. We watched it so hard that it swelled and heaved and bulged. But it was our eyes that did all the heaving.

We had a plan. If he were to roll aside the stone and arise we were going to make a big long welcoming speech, present him with a translation of 'Yes, we have no bananas' in Book of Kells style Celtic script, and then as there were thirty-five of us we were going to persuade him to remain in his new dimension. So, we waited.

Twilight descended until the rock blended with the hillside – there was no resurrection. Gratefully we eased ourselves towards the club. Just then a member brought our attention to some graffiti on the main cross. It was written in Old Irish and in old script. One of our many academics read it out: *gimigam fol cech nech*. He translated it as 'everything is a disguised banana'. There was no doubt about it, this was the Subject's message to humanity. We were so much in awe of its searing beauty that we almost went on our knees. In four little words it summed up all man wanted to know about mystery. This was no ordinary revealed secret but a weapon that, if set loose upon the wretched thought and philosophy of today, would wreak havoc among the minds of men and bring about the realisation of the Great Celtic Dream. But we are fond of our secrets and fonder still of our dreams and he who knows our secrets would surely tread on our dreams. And so we enacted that these precious words were classified and would be allowed only mingle in the minds of Oisín and Ó Maoil Íosa and all the countless heroes of the Gael till time and time were done.

The Immensity of War

When I was ten my mother died and my father was very upset because he couldn't look after both the horses and me. He was bad at that kind of thing, he said at the railway station as I took the train for a boarding school in the far west. It was an old castle run by a foreign religious order. An old monk gave us a tour. The Irish had owned it first, then the Normans and then the English. 'Castles very bad,' said the old monk, 'all fight and kill, not good.' He showed us a portrait of Lord Doonanar, the last owner, who one day during the Civil War had walked down the steps with an umbrella and an Airedale terrier, never to be seen again. The old monk took us along the battlements and pointed out the bullet holes in the walls. One very big hole had been made by a cannonball. He made each one of us in turn place our heads in the hole and feel the immensity of war.

Night does not fall on a castle. It comes up the steps and takes the place floor by floor, claiming as small change the straggling light of day on the turrets. And so we watched the spaces between our beds fill with night, our minds swaying to the rhythm of the yew trees. In the distant halls we heard the monks call to each other in guttural command.

The Matron inspected us. She was dark and foreign and, some of the boys thought, very beautiful. Her face was always flushed with some recent triumph in her war against her grubby charges. She held my head between her hands and peered closely at me. I smelt her perfume, I smelt the freshness of her clothes, I smelt Christmas day and breakfast in bed. After that I scrubbed my finger nails and cleaned my teeth five times a day, and polished my shoes until beads of sweat glistened on them. It paid off. One day she cradled my chin in her hands, smiled and said I was the cleanest boy in the castle.

I had a friend called Desmond, an American, who had failed to capture Matron's attention. The day his face and hands were right there would be something wrong with his shoes. He complained that she could never remember his name and always called him Damien. His parents had been killed in an automobile accident because his father was a real 'hot shot' driver. He loved to describe the wreckage. The fender of the car had finished up on top of a tree. Men gathered at the roadside to gaze up at the chrome glinting in the sun. He begged me to tell him about my father's horses but the question enraged me and I said I hated horses.

We studied Greek. The Classics monk, who wore a monocle, loved the Greeks, for they had been triumphant in all their wars. We studied Xenophon's *Anabasis*. The trials of his ten thousand troops skirmishing their way through deserts were matched by a roomful of boys who fought rearguard actions with the archaic syntax, and when they reached their destination and they gave vent to the famous cry *Thalatta, Thalatta,* the sea, the sea, we also took up the cry of exultation that meant the end of its wretched grammar. But there was to be no relief. We came to the city of Olynthus and the terrible fate that befell it: Philip had destroyed the city and sold all the citizens into slavery. 'The children also?' we asked. 'The men, women and children were sold in three separate lots,' he said. 'That was very wrong,' we said. 'In war, there is no wrong,' he said. 'We would agree in the case of the men, and even perhaps the women, but not the children. The children had done no wrong,' we countered. 'They were born in Olynthus,' he said. 'That wasn't fair,' we said. He said: 'There is no right and no wrong, there is merely good luck and bad luck.' We were confused and scared.

We took our food in the Great Hall. The monks' table was by the large fireplace where writing on the stonework said *In Hoc Signo Vinces* telling of some Irish clan who thought God was on their side. The monks took wine at their table, the cork popping and releasing to our noses the aromas of an older Europe full of laughing, victorious soldiers. But in distant lands wars were being fought. After dinner the monks would gather round the radio in the East Hall and listen to broadcasts in foreign tongues. We heard the crackling consonants rise in crescendo and watched the taut faces of the monks grow pale in the candlelight. Once the news was so important that dinner was late. The monks came silently into the Banqueting Hall and asked for our prayers in tense voices. The cold stone hurt our knees but the regularity of the litany eased our minds and it gave us strength to see big men take refuge among the small.

Once in the Spring my father came. His Mercedes pulled the horse-box through the gates and stopped at the bottom of the steps. I stood by the main door and though it was raining I held my cap in my hand. The Abbot warmly greeted my father, who wore a red feather in his hat. They both went around to the horse-box and peered through a chink in the door. Two monks dashed down the steps past me and did likewise. They all thought it was a beautiful horse. My father rolled up the collar of his coat and eyed the grey battlements and sodden greenery from under his hat. 'Yes,' he said, 'he is a fine horse but is easily upset. Rain especially upsets him.' 'Ja,' said the Abbot, 'here it is not good for ze horse, but in ze east of ze country it is arid, ja?'

My father put five pounds into my hand and patted my drenched head. He said I looked well, and the Abbot said we got everything we needed in the castle. I watched the car, encrusted with raindrops, swing through the gates towards the arid east where stallions could toss their manes in dry comfort.

Desmond would not believe that my father had visited me until I showed him the five pounds which the rain had turned to lettuce. He said I was mean with my father and that he would never talk to me again. He said he was fed-up with the castle because it was all about war and Ablative Absolutes and the monks always wore black. He would ask the First Bank of New England, whose ward he was, to send him back to a co-ed in America where there would be lots of pretty girls in pretty dresses and lady teachers nicer than Matron. At the mention of her name he grew enraged and said he hated being clean and threw himself on the horse dung in the paddock.

At night in the dormitory when I would awake I could hear the boys call out in their sleep to people who would never answer them again.

The Geography monk took us one wintry day through the castle. He said that though the castle had been built to cheat the west wind, the builders had failed because all the candles in the main hall

dripped on their east side. In such triumph he took us to the battlements where he tried to lecture us on the Ice Age. The rain soaked
our clothes and made the ink run in our copy books. Fog and mist
came tumbling down the glen, to be split in two by the castle, only
to join again at the bawn.

The wind took the words out of the monk's mouth, making him
almost roar. Out there somewhere there had been a glacier which
had ripped the glen out. We strained to imagine this cold architect
of glassy might; but the cold and wet made us grumble and one by
one we retreated down the tower. The monk was annoyed and, as
if to spite us, shouted after us that there was another Ice Age coming
and it would turn Ireland into a sand pit. We didn't care. Just before
he left he said, 'Crazy it vass to build a castle here, nozing to defend,
except Geography.'

In the Classics class we grew tired of Persian rearguards being cut
to pieces by Lacedemonian cavalry, we grew tired of triumph and
death. When we came to the Battle of Marathon we groaned. 'What
about the losers, we are tired of victory?' Desmond asked. 'The
losers lost and that's the end of them,' said the monk, 'we study the
good, the excellent.' 'The Irish lost,' said someone. 'My father was
Irish,' said Desmond. 'We never learned Irish,' we said. 'Greek is
the language of triumph, Irish is the language of defeat,' he said as
he adjusted his monocle. He strolled to the window and pondered
this new trend in his class. After a while he said, as if to himself, 'In
defeat too there can be dignity.' He turned towards us and said,
'Yes, it is true, too much victory is bad, a little defeat is good. The
Irish tongue is dark and deep and almost as difficult as Greek.' He
told us about an island nearby where a man lived who could speak
only Irish. But it was very sad because there was nobody to talk to,
everybody else had left. But we could all go out and meet this man
and go by boat and have a picnic. This news was followed by a
deafening cheer. For the rest of the week we could hardly sleep with
excitement.

The day came. The sun came out and the stonework soaked the
heat, shrinking the wintry heart of the castle. Matron smiled more
than usual and we all helped in making a hamper. Then, dressed in
red life-jackets, we filed down behind the Classics monk to the
harbour, all twelve of us. The sails were set and we glided out

beyond the headlands. Everything was a shade of blue, sky, ocean, island. We were true children of the universe and all we saw was ours. We crowded out at the little island slip. Beyond the slip was a deserted village. 'Who owns the houses?' we asked the monk. 'The inhabitants, they all go,' he said. 'Why did they go?' 'They were defeated,' he tapped his forehead. 'No fight.' He then went off in search of the old man.

We rummaged through the houses, tugging at doors and peering through windows. A chair was knocked over, a door banged, glass was broken, followed by silence and then laughter. Suddenly it was war, attackers and defenders. Doors were kicked and old furniture rammed into the breach. I, who had never broken anything in my life, found great pleasure in stripping the slates off a roof and throwing mortar at the defenders. Suddenly we all went on a rampage of destruction. Anything and everything that could be broken was smashed. It was Olynthus and I was Philip. I attacked a stairway with an old iron bar and made bits of it. Desmond was kicking and smashing old lobster pots. Somebody threw an old three-legged pot at a wall where it exploded into shards. It was the roaring of the Classics monk that brought us to our senses. Slowly, we all slunk out onto the street, like thieving curs. His monocle had dropped from his eye. He said it was a disgrace that boys from the castle could behave like this. He was ashamed and we would all get lines. Then we all trooped up the hill after him to the old man's cottage.

We entered a little house. There was a man sitting by the fire. He was big, old and ugly. There was a dog under the chair that looked dead. The monk took the only other chair at the fireside. There was a funny smell. Light could hardly get through the window because the net curtain was clogged with grime. Every place was dirty. We marvelled at the cracked cup and jugs on the dresser, and the old man was dressed in rags. Poverty was something we had read about only in books. Some of us sat on the table, others on the ground, but others stood because the floor was so dirty. 'Matron would do her nut here,' said Desmond.

The monk and the old man were talking in grunts. It must have been Irish. 'Let's give the old guy a couple of bucks and get out of here,' whispered Desmond. The monk motioned me to come and sit by the fire. I sat down beside the old man. The old man's fingernails were full of turf or something. His boots looked as if they were moored to the ground. The monk said Irish was a strange, mystical language. At about the time that Philip of Macedon had destroyed Olynthus, Irish was being spoken in Ireland. Now this man was the last in this province. He would now welcome us in his own tongue.

When he spoke his voice was deep like the beating of a drum, with guttural bits that would give you a sore throat. When he had finished, the monk told us that he would now sing an old song. Suddenly the man set up a wail that startled us. The monk nodded furiously at us as if to say: 'This is a song, like it.' The wail got worse, louder and longer. Sometimes he would stop and we would hope it was over, but no, he was just drawing breath, and he would come back with a throaty blast that made the dog wink. Most of his song went up the chimney.

Suddenly he grasped my hand in his, its calloused power startling me as much as the suddenness. It was like having your hand swallowed by a big hungry boot that couldn't find a foot. I saw the monk nod furiously at me and I guessed that this was part of the show. Both our hands vibrated on certain notes. I looked up at his face and into the dark privacy of his mouth, at the few yellow teeth that hung from his upper gum. Once I had seen a skull through a chink in a tomb. It seemed to snarl. I looked at the old man's face again and I saw the same snarl of death, either for himself or his language. And I knew then that being human was ugly and danger-ous. I was frightened and tugged my hand free. The singer stopped and everybody looked at me. Suddenly the door was flung open and the boatman shouted that the wind had changed and the weather could break at any minute. We all bolted for the door and made for the boat.

As we crossed the sound the boat began to pitch in the waves. I held on to the mast. The monk said I should be proud the old man had taken my hand. It was a custom. Anyway it must have been a long time since he had felt such a young hand. He droned on about the passing of races and cultures and even the headlands. Listening to him you would think the whole world was an ice cream on a hot day, melting fast. I held on to the mast, it was strong and powerful and wasn't dying. It was my best friend for the moment.

A New Eternity

The Potters had their village on the banks of the river which flowed from the setting sun into the mouth of the dawn. There were other villages but they were not important, for the Potters were arrogant and mouthy in their pride, scorning all who were not given to the cause of pottery.

There were different kinds – glass which stole colours out of the sun, china kind to the lips, tin as light as the air, stone solid, bronze with rings that chimed, and iron that feared neither hammer nor fire. They had their differences but all united under the common name of Potter.

In a hut in the centre of the village were kept the Tablets. These defined the art precisely and was their way of knowing when a pot was a pot. The Keeper of the Tablets was Potbelly, whose job involved acceptance or rejection of every new pot in accordance with the precepts of the Tablets. He was called this name because it was he who first hit upon the notion of making the body of a pot larger than the mouth, thus allowing for greater stuffing. As pots came Potbelly stamped them or added a comment or sent for the individual to tell him he had potential. Or he might chide him, pointing out his error in the Tablets. He rarely had to consult them for Potbelly found it easy to remember rules.

Every Blissday he published the pot of the week. This was done by placing the chosen pot on a stand outside his hut. All gathered to watch, for Blissday was a free day in the village. Some would dash around for a quick look just to make sure nobody had hit upon their idea. These would quickly depart, silent but glad. Others would clap their hands in appreciation. There might be passionate argument also. Potbelly listened carefully to this, nodding wisely at one side of the argument. But he stiffened when he heard accusations of bias, suggestions that his own friends appeared too often on the stand. Flowerpot was a good example. It was he who first discovered that by placing flowers in a pot a new dimension was added to art. Some potters stamped their feet when they saw Flowerpot on the stand again. They did the same for Potty. Once Potty hadn't enough tin to make her usual large pots. The result was a little vessel that pleased the women of the village greatly. Potty had grown rich and arrogant as a result.

The most angry of all the potters at the stand was Ket. He looked at the Pot of the Week and snarled, 'Rubbish, but polished rubbish. Pot polishers all of them – week after week. Where are the new constructions that are art?'

Potbelly heard him and winced.

'If you're so great,' said somebody, 'why don't you do better?'

Ket just stamped his foot and stalked off. To bring his girl, Goldipots, into the forest or something. (It was a great honour in the village to have a pot-name. No sooner had she reached puberty than the name suggested itself.)

'When are you going to have a work accepted – not to mention making the stand?'

He took her by the shoulders and his eyes gazed deep into her. 'I'm better than any of them. Don't worry, I'll show them yet. I have great pots down here,' he said, thumping his chest. She put her ear to his breast and listened.

'I hear something beating,' she said. 'Is it a heart or a pot?' and they both laughed in rare communion. But she was never sure of him.

But the great oaks of the forest also knew the snarling dogs of his soul. Many a time he had screamed at the trees as he should have done with Potbelly. He was weary of rejection. Nobody would listen to him. Arguing with Potbelly was a waste of time.

'A pot is a pot is a pot. Send me a pot, you dolt.'

'This is a pot.'

'A pot with no hangers?'

'Hangers would have destroyed the symmetry of this pot.'

'Heresy!' shouted Potbelly, and he brought Ket over to the Tablets. 'I quote the Word as it has been handed down. Tablet 3,

Verse 5. It is written that a pot shall possess hangers (or their equivalent) in order to give a pot its final worthiness. A pot that lacks hangers (or their equivalent) is null and void. There now,' said Potbelly.

'Manure!' screamed Ket.

'Sacrilege!' roared Potbelly. 'I'll call the council and have you flogged for insulting the Tablets. Worse, I'll have you banished.'

Ket paled and choked out an apology.

'You're a disgrace to your honoured father, Poteen.'

And he was. His father was humiliated. He had never been an exceptional potter but he had invented the drink that bore his name. Each night in the drinking huts he was toasted.

'Goodness, you have me disgraced, son, why can't you make an honest pot?'

'I've made hundreds,' Ket said, wearily.

'Rubbish! Do you call a pot made of oak wood a pot, do you? As soon as you put it on the fire the wretched thing goes up in smoke, you dolt!'

'Well, don't put it on the fire.'

'Don't talk like that, you know what the Tablets say. Tablet 6, Verse 12. Fire is to the pot as man is to woman. A pot that withstands not the fire is null and void. And Great Forge in the Sky, you had the cheek to send to my esteemed colleague, Potbelly, a pot that had no mouth and no cover.'

'Maybe it wasn't a pot then. Maybe it was a thing,' Ket muttered in despair.

'It wasn't a thing, it was a pot,' roared Poteen. 'Everything is a pot except some of them are null and void. And no mouth. Tablet 7, Verse 3. A pot shall possess a mouth and a lid, for it is written that all things shall have their openings and closings. Did you hear that?'

Ket walked out and banged the door loudly behind him.

A cold breeze blew in from the Great Plain. It made him feel lonely. He moved aimlessly into the centre of the village. There he stopped. Night was coming on. He listened. Tap-tap, every forge sent out the same message – tap-tap – this is creation – tap-tap – this is eternal knowledge being beaten into shape. He shuddered. He was afraid – afraid of knowledge, afraid of shape, and the eternity between them. He faced the wind and the oncoming night and said defiantly: 'It is I, and only I, that can break that eternity.'

He walked into Spoon's forge. Spoon was his friend. One day he had made a tiny pot with a long handle. Potbelly went wild when he saw it. He quoted the Tablets. A pot had to have two handles.

'And now,' said his friend, 'up in Potbelly's there's a two-handled spoon under glass, although the villagers prefer one handle.'

'Spoon, what will I do?' said Ket in desperation.

'Don't break the rules – pretend to keep them,' was the answer.

Ket wasn't satisfied. The inner terms of proportion rejected such sophistry. He wandered down to Skillet's. He was very old but wily, and he liked Ket.

'Skillet, I feel I'm going to cry. I'm at my limit.'

'Cry then, I wish I could, it's a sign you're young and alive, my son.'

'Skillet, I feel deep down that I have some great pots.'

'And so you have, and so you have.'

'But nobody wants them. They laugh at me.'

'Patience, Ket. Give things time. Be sly.'

Ket felt the rage overflow. 'Do you know what?' he said. 'I feel likegoing up and smashing all the Tablets. Make smithereeens of them.'

'Smash nothing but dint everything,' came the drowsy reply.

'What does that mean?'

But the old man had fallen asleep.

He strode through the forest. His jaunty gait, the towering trees, and now and again the casual moonlight on his eyes, stirred up old shadows of his soul. He felt a terrible mood take hold of him. The mood of a pot being born. He raced back to his forge, pumped the bellows, blowing white heat through the embers. All night and all next day he hammered and tapped on the anvil. The people heard and shook their heads.

That evening he emerged from his forge with a bundle under his arm. He looked haggard but had a strange calmness about him. He went into Potbelly's hut and flung the bundle on the table.

'There!' he said, in a note of triumph. Potbelly looked pained.

'Ket, I'm tired. I want to go to bed. Won't it do tomorrow?'

'Not this.' Ket's eyes gleamed. 'Go on, open it.'

Potbelly shrugged and opened the bundle. For a long time he

stared.

'What is it?' he asked, horrified.

'It's a pot, but a different pot,' came the reply. Potbelly walked all around the table three times, gazing on the strange pot of gleaming tin.

'What did you put that on it for. What is it?'

'It's a pipe,' said Ket, 'I call it a spout.'

'A what?'

'A spout. You know the way water spouts.'

Potbelly glared at him, then quickly back at the pot.

'You know what you've done, you've made a filthy pot, a dirty pot. I've never seen the like of it before.'

Ket looked at him in amazement. 'Whatever do you mean?' he said. 'If you incline this pot to one side the water comes out the spout.'

Potbelly looked aghast. He ran over to the pot, bent forward and squinted down the spout. 'This thing is a hole,' he said with an air of discovery.

'Well, a spout,' said Ket.

'A hole, a damned pothole, a hole in a pot, you dolt.'

'A spout.'

'A long pot hole,' said Potbelly in rage. 'Tablet 16, Verse 5. A pothole is the incarnation of evil. Let them be accursed. Heresy! The man has built a pot with a pot-hole in it.'

'Alright,' said Ket, 'it's a long pot-hole but it's best for pouring water.'

'Pour! Did you say "pour"? Tablet 9 Verse 11: to remove liquid from pot, remove lid, incline pot and pour over edge. Alternative method – procure pot of smaller dimensions and bail accordingly. There now.'

'That's it,' roared Ket. 'With my pot there's no need for messing like that.'

Potbelly groaned. He walked all round the room, holding his head and all the time he muttered: 'What will I do, he's going to get flogged or banished. And I must save him for the sake of his father.

Suddenly he got an idea and his face brightened. He took Ket by the shoulders. 'You know, this is a most sacriligious pot. Now go home, cut off that dirty thing with your file, put three legs under it, weld on the hangers, and I'll pass it. I will, by heaven. Think of it, your first valid pot.'

Ket hardly heard Potbelly. He looked vacantly past the Keeper, at a point where time and space wouldn't know each other and he was filled with wonder; for the old eternity he had known so long had now gone.

'Maybe, Potbelly, it isn't a pot at all,' he said.

Potbelly erupted.

'Everything is a pot, but some of them are null and void, null and void, do you hear?' and he bundled the contraption into Ket's hands and pushed him towards the door.

'Heretic!' he screamed with tears in his eyes. As he pushed him out the door he added with venom, 'and you have insulted the women of this village also, you wretch.'

The doorbang carried all the way to the river.

Next day the village awoke to the banging of hammer on wood. It was Ket building something. All day he hammered and it wasn't until evening that people could see what he was erecting outside his door.

'He's making a stand like Potbelly's,' someone said suddenly. The gathering was rooted to the ground with shock.

Someone tittered, then somebody laughed outright. Soon the whole village shuddered with suppressed glee. 'Here comes Potbelly,' someone shouted, and the crowd held its breath. He came waddling down the street, his face purple. He stood in front of the stand. Three times he opened his mouth but only gurgles could be heard. He wheeled about and thumped back up the street, snorting.

Quietly the crowd faded away for Potbelly had suggested the theme, the tempo he had left up to themselves.

It was Blissday morning and a funny pot appeared on Ket's stand. All day the people came to see it but only in ones and twos.

There were no comments – none. Women and children darted nervous glances at it and hurried off.

Goldipots came and looked wide-eyed at it. His heart beat fast as he searched her face. He would give a lot if she would only smile. He would almost give his pot – almost.

'Why did you have to do this to us?' she hissed.

'Do what?' he was crushed.

'Make a fool of yourself and me.'

She came close to him and her expression changed. Her beautiful eyes pleaded. 'Throw it in the river, now, do it for me.'

'Never,' was his simple answer. She turned away from him and she moved through the street, each step walking on his heart.

All day he sat, all day in silence, all day in hurt. Potbelly hadn't come. Towards evening he tried to tell himself it was a beginning. Towards sunset the village was unusually quiet. Where was everybody? Nothing stirred.

He heard her feet first madly thumping the dust, then she shot out of a side street, towards him, scared as scared could be. 'Run, Ket, into the mouth of the dawn,' she blurted and just as suddenly she was gone. There was no time to consider, for just then the streets blackened with the cloaks of men. Behind them came the women, each eye an enemy – all silent.

Ket stood up and tried to smile.

'Fellow potters, I welcome you. This is not really a pot, it is a vessel that . . . – '

Old Crackpot jumped out in front, his jaw almost out of joint with anger. 'What is the meaning of this insult?' he screamed. Ket chose to ignore him.

'If you incline this vessel, the water comes . . . '

Potty jumped forward and tapped the spout with her finger.

'What's that?' she said.

'Oh, this I call a spout – the water pours through this spout beautifully.' He tried to keep calm. The women began to hiss, their eyes locked on the solitary potter. Flowerpot spoke out: 'He has defiled not only our Tablets but our womanhood too.'

Ket spluttered. 'What are you talking about? This vessel . . .'

'Heretic!' someone screamed, and a stone flew through the air and struck his forehead. Blood flowed down both sides of his nose.

'Now please, just a minute, I just . . . '

'Filth!' The cry was as sharp as the two stones that struck his face and put him staggering to the wall of his forge. He fell to the ground and tasted the salt of his own blood, the salt of fear. The crowd towered above him, dark and powerful.

'Please, fellow potters,' he pleaded, 'I merely wished to

demonstrate . . . ' They tasted his fear.

'Kill him!' The cry was taken up about the street. The men drew their cudgels and cut down the fallen potter until the last shiver had left his flesh forever. They threw his body on the bonfire they had prepared. They watched the smoke, satisfied.

'Throw in the infernal pot,' said Potbelly. But nowhere was it to be found. 'Never mind,' he said, 'The Tablets have been avenged.

Late that night Skillet and Spoon were alone in the forge. A small square of window let in the ancient starlight. Skillet held ther funny pot in his hand, pouring drink into glasses without spilling a drop.

'What shall we call the pot?' 'A Ket? A Ketter? A Kettle?' said Spoon as he took his glass.

Skillet only chuckled.

'Ket is dead,' said Spoon. 'Let us drink to Ket.'

'Ket is dead but his art lives,' said Skillet.

'Then let us drink to his art,' said Spoon.

'New art creates a new eternity,' said Skillet.

'Then let us drink to that,' said Spoon.

And they did. For a new eternity was born.

Waiting for Dev

The horses stood in the cold, riders hunched in saddles. They were cobs on a day off from the drudgery of the hills. Calloused hocks and wealed backs told of tight swingletrees and careless straddling. All they wanted was a wall to lean against. All were silent in the cold. Nobody took any notice as a big grey's splashing urine foamed among the heavily fetlocked hooves.

But deep inside Cashman's store, Dan Kerns saw it, and it made him wonder all the more about the horsemen. They had suddenly clattered up out of the back lanes, filling the street with the sound of steel on stone. Horses meant either funerals or politics. But nobody was dead. He backed farther in among the wine casks; in his hand a brass funnel yielded up its sheen to the polish. Dan Kerns' workmate, Mike Spring, was decanting port from a keg. Suddenly, his name was called from the street, 'Mike!' Mike got up and sauntered out to the leader of the horsemen. Dan Kerns listened to the muttering and his hand tightened on the funnel. Mike Spring strolled back in, an embarrassed grin on his face. 'Dan, the volunteers want more paraffin. The last drop stood no ground. Maybe we could give them a little more.' Dan dropped the funnel, stalked to the doorway and gazed out at the throng. 'Volunteers you say – they're too young ever to have fired a shot – volunteers for what?' Mike Spring shrugged. 'You know, volunteers – sure they're all over the place.'

'We were volunteers once, you and I.'

'We were.'

'What did we volunteer for?'

'To fight for Irish freedom.'

'We got that nineteen years ago. Now what have they volunteered for?' He gestured at the huddling animals and men. Mike Spring came over to have another look at them. 'They', he said, 'have volunteered for the crack.' Dan Kerns, who had been an officer in the Troubles, almost spat on the ground. 'The crack?' 'Yes,' said Mike, 'and the torchlight procession for Dev.'

'For Dev?'

'Yeh.'

'They look like turfcutters at a funeral in Scartaglin.'

'They call themselves the Coolforran Volunteers,' said Mike.

'More paraffin you say. And who's going to pay for it? Billy the Kid out there?' They both looked at Ned Landers sitting awkwardly astride his Irish Draught, a great black coat giving him a sinister look.

'There's a war on, Mike, Hitler has already pissed through the Low Countries, God only knows where next he's heading.'

'I suppose he'll head for the High Countries now,' said Mike helpfully.

Dan laughed. 'What do they want so much paraffin for?'

'For practice. The horses aren't used to processions.'

'Cashman will miss it. The stuff is rationed.'

'It's not everyday Dev comes to town.'

He should say 'no' outright, but it was only the second most dangerous word in the town, 'yes' being the first. They turned back into the store. 'What time will Dev be here?' Mike Spring closed one eye, aimed the other at some point in the sky, as if knowledge could be shot out of the air like wild duck. 'He's coming from the west, so he'll be delayed there. About six I'd say.' Mike Spring stood in the doorway exactly half-way between his chosen career among the barrels and his dreams among the horsemen. Thus he would always be, thought Dan Kerns, never making contact with either. Dan shrugged, 'O.K., it's the least we can do for the Chief, I suppose.'

Mike shot over to the barrel of paraffin in the corner and began to ladle it into a bottle which he took to the street and doused the sod of turf that each rider had mounted on a hayfork. There was silence as he moved from one to another, like a priest, nodding, sprinkling, nodding, sprinkling. Dan Kerns retreated to the back of the store. This was a recent habit of his, as if he could draw strength from the Mediterranean sun locked within the barrels. As he watched the

roadway from the shadows, he liked to review his life, his forty-five
years of diminishing favour with the world, from Dan Kerns the
county footballer, to rebel, to officer, outlaw, victor, farm labourer,
father, reader of James Connolly by candlelight, and now polisher
of brass funnels.

Ned Landers, the leader of the horsemen, nudged his horse with
kicks on the flanks up onto the footpath, where he addressed his
men. This was the most Republican town in Ireland and the
welcome for DeValera would have to be in keeping with that tradition. When his car entered the town they were going to escort it in
two lines, with pikes blazing. To practice this operation, he drew
them up in two lines. The commotion of hooves while he did this
sounded like showers of buckets on the roadway. The lighting
torches sent shadows leaping about the street, telling of approaching twilight. Dan Kerns remained among the kegs, his eyes in
twinkle with the brasses. It was all too much for one old grey that
suddenly shied, backed his rump into the door, and slammed it
against some barrels. The torch fell from the hand of the rider and
a shower of sparks jumped into the store. Dan Kerns raced for the
paraffin drum and slammed the lid on it. He turned on Mike.

'This is bad work. If Cashman hears about this there'll be trouble.
It's not the paraffin – it's this lot out here.'

Mike knew what he meant. Two bloody years of civil war after
independence had left so much spite in the town that all the barrels
and kegs of the store could not hold it. Like the adder in Shakespeare it was the bright day that brought it forth, and craved wary
walking. Or politicians. The name DeValera could split families in
two, neater than you'd slice loaves. Mike shrugged and said there
were things a man had to do.

'We've done our bit, think of yourself, think of Cashman,' hissed
Dan Kerns.

'We live in each others shadows,' was all the reply Dan got. Mike
had always been the same, governed by heart only, head provided
proverbs and comments on the weather. Heart the master, head the
apprentice. Life was a condition not to be thought but to be felt right
up to the last moment. When they were on the run it was only
natural that Mike should collect a bucket of eggs from the farms and
boil them, oil their guns, run messages to their girlfriends,

clean out a tomb before allowing the leader in to sleep in it, going on horseback to a distant pub for two quarts of stout, playing the mouth organ for them while on forced marches.

A cold wind blew in from the sea that set the horses pawing the ground. The odd snowflake sailed past the doorway of the store. Outside in the street a cork popped, then teeth on the jowl of a bottle. Ned Landers sent the whiskey on its round, each man wiping it with his sleeve. When it was empty Ned showed what generals are made of. 'Who's for a Woody?' says he, flashing the green box of twenty Woodbines. They were so scarce that even non-smokers took one. Then with heels jabbing the flanks of his horse, he went from rider to rider, a British army-issue lighter clicking under each fag.

Mike Spring went out again with the bottle of paraffin, drenching new sods, spilling some on the ground. 'Easy on, Mike, there's a war on, this might be the last barrel,' said Dan Kerns. His words carried easily on the frosty air. Ned Landers heard them. 'This war won't last pissing time, no worry, no worry,' he said. Everybody looked at him. 'Look,' said Ned, 'Hitler went down through Holland like shit through a goose. He did the same to Belgium. Those Belgians are fuckin' useless.'

'Are they Ned?' said Thady Chute.

'They wouldn't bate soldiers off their sisters. Well, he'll do the same to France, then wan crack at d'English and – snap – you'll have paraffin flowing down the main street.'

Dan Kerns was irritated. These boys were young but did they have to be stupid? War to them was a stray word in their father's speech, death the kick of a horse. For Dan, war meant many different things– but mainly the ambush of Leaba na Bó. When the shotguns had finished blasting the Crossley tender into the ditch the white thorn blossom, so frail, was dislodged by the sound and it fell with each echo onto the bloodied soldiers. That blossom falling through his mind was the quietest thing in the universe.

Ned Landers, though in his twenties, sat on the saddle like Gabby Hayes with piles. Snowflakes began to winnow down the street. Jamesy Quilter from the foundry passed up. He stopped in amazement to look at the horsemen. Then with disgust on his face, he walked on.

'He's one of 'em,' said Tadhg Hannafin.

'One of who?'

'A Blueshirt.'

'A Blueshirt? Hey, you fuckin' shirt you,' Paaty Diggins shouted after him.

Jamesy Quilter turned and made a rude pelvic gesture. Suddenly Ned Landers opened his big black coat and took out a double-barrel. There was a tremendous explosion and the horses scattered like sparks from a fire, trampling each others heels to escape. One bolted in among the barrels and began lashing out at everything. 'Christ get him out,' roared Dan Kerns.

'Jesus Christ, help me,' roared a rider, whose horse had fallen on top of him. There was a terrible commotion trying to free him. They finally got him free and he was dragged off to a pub to be revived. Slowly the other horses began to canter back, their ungainly legs delivering hammer blows to the street. They gathered round their leader who was statuesque on his own horse, smoking gun in hand.

'Honour o' Christ, what're you tryin' to do to us, Landers?'

Landers looked very surprised, then slowly he began to grin. 'Christ, lads, I pissed in my pants.' The whole company began to laugh.

'Twas an accident,' said he, climbing down off his horse. He walked into the store. 'Have you any hay, Kerns?' Dan Kerns looked at him with both satisfaction and mockery. 'The shot made you piss in your pants?' But Ned wasn't listening, he was packing hay down inside his trousers. Then he was up on his horse again.

'Tell you what lads, we blew smut off that Blueshirt.' There was a laugh here and there.

'They're getting scarce now, the Blueshirts,' said Micheál McEllistrum.

'If I had anything to do with them they'd be as scarce as rocking horse's shit,' said Ned.

Two Guards came up the street to them. They were not in step, and this destroyed any chance of military presence. They stopped at the edge of the horsemen. Neither was sure just how fierce they should look. One of them piped up: 'Was there a shot fired here?' said he. There was a tense silence. Then Ned answered. 'That was Mikey Bunion's horse farting.' Some of the riders almost fell off their horses with mirth. The two Guards strode away redfaced, doing their best to keep in step. Ned was in charge again. Dan Kerns was livid with Ned Landers; all that was needed to lead this bunch was the right brand of vulgarity. They began to joke and rib each other. One of them noticed Dan Kerns' sourness.

'Hey, Kerns, weren't you in the G.P.O. in 1916?'

'Oh, he was,' said somebody, 'getting a dog licence.' The whole group burst out laughing. Dan Kerns drew himself up to his former officer's height and marched crisply out to the middle of the street. He came to a military halt sharply. 'There will always be free hay here, for the Coolforran Volunteers, the next time they piss in their pants,' he said.

But Ned never got a chance to reply for suddenly a horseman rode up the street at a furious pace, shouting that Dev had entered by the shortcut and would probably beat them to the stand. Ned never waited for a second but spurred his horse forward and barely made it to the head of the group as they wheeled madly about, and galloped off towards the centre of the town, each rider trailing a few yards of flame.

Dan and Mike turned back into the store. The draymen would be there in the morning. It was five o'clock but dark, and candles had to be lit. It was cold but cold makes you work harder. Soon the store was agurgle with taps and syphons, stout gulping from barrels, sherry discreetly pouring, barley wine whispering into small bottles, soda water hissing.

'What's on in Breen's tonight?'

Mike knew instantly. '*The Song of Bernadette* – religion,' he said.

'What's on in Foley's?'

'Roy Rogers, and Gene Autrey.'

'Jesus, I thought Cagney was supposed to be on in Foley's.'

'The car ran out of petrol in Baanteer. Cagney will spend the night in Baanteer.'

'This war is a bastard.' To do without petrol was bad for some, but to do without James Cagney was bad for all.

'Yes, fuck Hitler.'

'There was a good show on Tuesday night in Breen's, *Tarzan and the Secret of Zostra*.'

'Good, was it?'

'Bloody great,' said Mike, 'about thirty blacks got et be crocodiles. The fuckin' screams outa them could be heard in the market.'

'I'm for Cagney myself,' said Dan.

'Yes,' said Mike, 'do you remember the night he came into the pub in Chicago, and stood just inside the door?'

'I do well.'

'They knew, the whole lota them knew. By Christ, they were scared. Then he pulled out a tommy-gun and shot the bloody lot of them. Edward G. Robinson got it in the belly. It took him about three minutes to die though. Edward G. is one ugly looking bastard.'

'That's the way to do it.'

'By God,' said Mike, 'if we had a gun like that the night we were ambushed in Skreen – there'd have been a different story to tell. Do you know what, I was so scared that night I ran up a blackthorn tree and when it was over I couldn't come down. Fright is funny too – if you live.'

Dan Kerns straightened up aid said, 'Betty Grable.'

'Ah yes, Betty Grable.'

Dan looked down at his hands – they were blue with the cold.

'Hedy Lamarr,' said Mike.

'Hedy Lamarr,' said Dan Kerns softly and looked about the flickering kegs, and out at the square darkness of the doorway beyond which the promise of the revolution contrived to brave out its disappointment in threadbare penury.

Mike threw down his funnel. 'I'm tired of this – this is no life. Three pounds six and eight pence per week and the pint is eight pence. And now this income tax crowd want a shilling in the pound.'

Dan nodded.

'And,' continued Mike, 'today is a national occasion. I should be down there giving a hand.'

Dan nodded again.

'And,' said Mike, 'seven o'clock is no knocking-off time for a civilized man.'

Dan Kerns walked over to him and laid a hand on his shoulder. 'You fire ahead, Mike, I'll cover for you.'

Mike's face beamed. 'Great man, would you? I might even ask

Dev for your coat.'

Dan Kerns had once placed his coat on DeValera's shoulders as he harangued a crowd in the pouring wet of Castlemaine. Later Dan heard that it was being worn by a volunteer in the Rathmore area. He had sent a dispatch rider to claim it, but the rider had been shot in Barradubh. It had been a leather coat with brass buttons, which he still missed in moments of vanity.

Mike slunk off, duty and loyalty both tugging his face into frowns of doubt and smiles of conviction. Even Dan felt the pull of old loyalty as he watched him; but he wasn't tempted. He had become wary of causes – they were the second most troublesome item in life after T.B. And of late, Dan had come to recognize that there were two types of people in life: one, those who became embroiled in a cause; two, those who sidestepped it.

It would be very easy to meet the first kind this evening by following Mike: men who slept in graveyards with him, men who were excommunicated from the Church and were refused Communion at the altar with him, men who blew bridges and derailed trains with him, men who thought they were fighting for a revolution. But the spoils of rebellion are rarely delivered up to the simple rebel. Nothing was delivered except the confusion that must come the day after victory and liberty; and afterwards the bitterness which would mark their countenances for life. In their cups the talk would drift back to the old days of valley, mountain, and ambush, to the day I was nearly executed, to the time you made the mad dash with the Mills bombs to Barr na Binne, to the time we all spent the night in Kelleher's hayshed and Johneen set it on fire with his pipe – and all the while they waste the passion of their eyes on sinking pints.

And the second type? He envied them. Those who, having helped to free one country, immediately set about looking for another to live in. No civil war for them – to a man today they were in America. Fergus Booley, the Lewis gun expert, now Fire Brigade Chief in Springfield, Mass., Eamonn Cuneen and Sean Lawlor both building contractors in Boston. And his own brothers, all high up in the New York Police, and they never stopped begging him to come over for good. But Philomena knew that cities in America were evil and she would shake her head vehemently at the suggestion, while she hung out pink anoraks and blue and yellow lumberjackets to dry; the annual hand-me-downs from his brothers in America, but in colours that told of a different freedom.

Yes he was sick of rebellions, war and revolutions. The worst of it was the rate at which they were forgotten – for generations grew up thicker and faster than ragwort; people who had no time for echoes. And the old comrades meeting once in a while to borrow the remaining bullets from each other to shoot old horses or sick dogs. And a medal, which visitors to the house bit with their teeth to test for silver. God, did all revolutions end like that?

'Who's been spreadin' all the horse shit around here?' Cashman stood in the doorway arms akimbo, a large man with his back to Dan, blocking the little light already there. Dan Kerns got up and walked out to him. The road was indeed in a bad way. Sparrows were already working through dung for undigested seeds. 'Shenanigans, that's what it is, Dan, shenanigans.' He turned into the store and stopped, his nose quivering. He had a nose so keen that he could smell how much port or sherry had been spilled. He sniffed again and frowned. 'Is it all tapped?'

'Just enough for three days I'd say.'

Cashman had two buckets of liquid in his hands. 'I brought ullage, Guinness ullage for the horses. 'Twould shine old boots for you. Mike gone?'

'I sent him out on a message.'

'Did you now. I thought I saw him down the street stuck in that riff-raff.'

'Are you sure it was him?'

'I'd know that face back to front in a fog.'

Poor old Mike, if a stone fell off a castle, 'tis on Mike it would fall, Dan thought.

'Here, here, let's have one look at the horses,' said Cashman.

They moved through the barrels to the back of the store where two large Clydesdales munged oats out of chew. Cashman danced around them, petting them, tickling their ears, with soothing guttural words. He took a fist of oats and let it trickle through his fingers. 'There's enough dust in that to break an elephant's wind.'

He settled himself in a manger full of hay between the two munging, jerking heads.

'You might as well sit,' he said magnanimously. Dan sat on an old butter box. Cashman chose a straw with care and began to nibble it, then examine the chewed end, as if for portents. 'This town is full of blackguards; they'd run through galloping horses for drink, and the best of them hardly know night from day. Their wretchedness will be the end of us all.' Cashman had been a commandant in the Free State Army, while Dan had been an officer on the opposing Republican side. They respected each other though never spoke about the war or politics, but the private anguish of the hard-working patriot always leaked out of Cashman's words.

'They're starving in Scolb Lane and in the cloisters,' said Dan Kerns evenly.

'If they got up off their arses and got busy, they wouldn't have time to starve.' All that remained of Cashman's military training was rapid clipped speech. 'Twenty years ago this country was humming – there was law, there was order, there was sweat, toil, and satisfaction – now it's a free-for-all – things are falling apart. Two out of every ten men I meet are as upright as the sun – as for the rest they are furze – pure furze. Don't spend a threepenny-bit on them.'

'Are you saying the fight for freedom wasn't worth it?' asked Dan. Cashman sucked his straw and eyed far away vistas in his mind. 'The fight was fought because it had to be done. We were young and that's that. We also got married because we were young. Whether things turn out good or bad doesn't matter this traneen,' and he cast the straw out of his mouth. One of the things that Kerns admired about Cashman was that he was one of the few of the monied class who threw in his lot with the fight in 1918-21. Dan Kerns had already noted that most of the men who fought and risked were the cobblers, tailors, farm-labourers – men who had nothing but dreams. Well, they held on to their dreams only to see them turn sour, like milk, in the thunder of liberty. According to James Connolly things were going to be different. They were going to share – like the land. Well they didn't share anything, and as soon as they got liberty they banned the writings of Connolly. So Dan Kerns was confused.

Cashman was squinting up at the roof. 'It isn't this but that,' he said, 'd'you see that roof, it's going to fall any one of these days on the poor horses. Sometimes I think I'm going to have to sell this

place. Things are getting tight. This damn war is as long as tomorrow, and stuff is vanishing off the market. Money is running as thin
as water. Which brings me to the matter of Mike. We'll have to part
– I haven't a thing against him – but this store won't carry two men
any more.'

Their eyes looked everywhere but at each other. Dan's hand
toyed with the broken hinge of the door.

'If you could stand your ground here on your own there'd be an
extra guinea a week for you in it. Twenty-wan shillings will buy an
awful lot of jam. You're the man could do it.'

Dan didn't speak. Greed was pushing up from somewhere in his
throat. He felt like cat before the theft. Philomena would lose her
mind; furniture, bikes for the kids. His hand tightened on the hinge.

'You sure about Mike, he's a good man?'

'A good man, when there's no need for a good man, might as well
be a bad man,' Cashman said with the ruthless logic of the
businessman.

'Now,' said Cashman slowly, 'give me your answer, now.'

Dan thought about Mike for a second. There were other stores in
the town. He'd manage. There was so much tension that the horses
stopped chewing. Dan wet his lips. 'I'll take it,' he said of a rush. He
hated himself for wetting his lips.

'Right then,' said Cashman, jumping down from his perch, 'the
Chamber of Commerce is having a parade at the end of the month.
I want the two Clydesdales drawing the drays at the head of the
show. You'll have to sieve their oats and give it to them washed.'
The responsibility for horses had been Mike's, Dan hated them.

'Tell Kelleher, the farrier, that they are to be shod proper this
time, not with roller skates like the last time. I want them clipped
and curried. Oil their hooves and harness and, oh, yes, don't forget
the Brasso – every one of them going up the town as neat as two little
girls the day of a Feis. Understand?'

'Yes.' He was going to earn this guinea. But it wasn't that –
something else was bothering him – a new thought was attacking
him like a dog savaging a sheep. Cashman led him through the old
musty passages at the back. Shouting out orders and directions for
this and that, holes, leaks, doors. But life was suddenly becoming
transparent for the first time in Dan Kern's life. He would now have

to build a house. Each shovelful would be like digging his own grave. A house would be another knot. That guinea would hang him.

'There will be a bottling machine delivered here on Saturday night – you wouldn't mind being here to receive it?' Goodbye Cagney and Bogart. Here come many, many years of pink lumberjackets. Suddenly he knew a second-hand New York every Saturday night was no longer any use to him – he wanted the real thing. Between Philomena and Cashman he would be castrated. He licked his lips again, mind racing. How could he ever face Ned Spring again?

The store was full of tea and sugar. Cashman had seen the war coming – for his eye measured life, not for length but for shortage. 'Every box and chest must be tinned on the outside – vermin they are everywhere. And new locks on all the doors.'

'For vermin?' asked Dan Kerns.

'And spillage – there's more drink spilled here in a day than at a wedding in Lyracrumpane. No more spillage.'

And this town – what the hell did it mean to him. The routine at the store, a few pints if he was lucky, a glance at the excitement of others on the odd Saturday night, the penny pinching at home, the kids that day by day were turning out like the neighbours he despised. And this bloody war. They'd be invaded.

'Paddy Cashman, I've a question to ask you – you're a man who understands war, people, things – much better than I do.'

Cashman squinted at him suspiciously but there was neither mockery nor flattery in Kern's words. 'Yes,' he said proudly.

'How long is this war going to last?' Dan asked. Cashman thought for a moment.

'The battle is toughening and the skies are rattling in our direction. Whichever crowd comes we won't last porridge time. Could be years. Every man for himself and those at the bottom in a bowl of trouble.'

Cashman was right. Kerns had come through two wars and though he won out he might as well have been throwing snowballs – for all he gained. But he'd never make it through a third. In his heart he knew he was a volunteer type, and he feared it – for the end of such hearts was to shelter under a marble slab. Paddy Cashman was at the doorway again, his nose quivering suspiciously.

'Paraffin!'

'What?'

'Don't you smell it? Paraffin!'

Cashman looked at him, as it began to dawn on him, and marched over to the drum. 'Christ, it's nearly all gone?' Dan didn't tell him that his quarryman had taken thirty gallons that morning which wouldn't show on the book till Saturday.

He marched back to Dan, fire in his eyes. 'There was enough there to last ten families for a year – where did it go?'

Kerns drew himself up to his full height. 'I think it's only right to tell you that you volunteered it for the cause.'

Cashman looked out at the roadway, then at the drum, then back to Dan. 'What cause?' he asked quietly.

'The cause of freedom – the cause of Destiny.' The word destiny had been commandeered by the followers of DeValera. It was not lost on Cashman. And then Dan added: 'You gave it "Do chum glóire dé agus onóra na hÉireann – For the glory of God and the honour of Ireland".' This was the motto of DeValera's new newspaper *The Irish Press*. Cashman absorbed the information and candles began to light in his eyes until they blazed. But there was a war on and Cashman was not a squanderer, not of even the passion of his eyes. The candles quenched and the ice took over. He put out his hand.

'The key,' he said quietly.

Dan Kerns pulled out the brass key that had not left his possession in years, and handed it over. It was a ceremony, silent, because they both knew its formula.

'Drop in to Mrs Parson's,' were Cashman's last words. She was his book-keeper.

Dan Kerns put on his yellow lumberjacket, and walked down the street more free than at any time since his childhood. He called into Willy Joe Hegarty's pub and settled himself on a stool. Somewhere he heard the clatter of hooves, and the notes of a band. Outside the window snowflakes fell as slowly as old memories through the mind. All old memories should fall like snowflakes, should become slush, should vanish in the fires of Spring, for each year brought its promise, and memories and promise do not mix.

On the wall there was a picture of the *Queen Elizabeth* ploughing its way through the Atlantic. He smiled at it as if it were an old friend, and he felt a selfish calm take hold of his bones. Then he had a Paddy. Then he ordered another and another.